WHEN A MAN LOVES A WOMAN

WHEN A MAN LOVES A WOMAN

Many a man proclaims his own steadfast love, but a faithful man who can find? The righteous walks in integrity— blessed are his children after him!

Proverbs 20:6-7 ESV

Taiwo Iredele Odubiyi

PRAISES FOR THE BOOKS OF TAIWO IREDELE ODUBIYI

Your Excellency Sir, good day to you. I just finished reading two of your sister's books on Kindle ... Taiwo Odubiyi. Even though I wasn't completely sure of the name, the style was very much recognizable. It's her, right? I still enjoy her style and content, very genuine and true to the circumstances – *Mrs. Faith Ekwekwuo, Senior Nigerian Diplomat*

Pastor, you are a blessing to me....I always consider your works as special gifts to me. I mentioned this to a bookshop clerk "I prefer spending my money on this woman's books than clothes." Your works have opened my eyes to a lot of things. From your books, I get answers to questions that bother my mind. You are a special kind of angel sent to both singles and married couples. YOU MADE ME KNOW THAT EVERY RELATIONSHIP AND MARRIAGE MUST HAVE CHRIST AS THE PILLAR AND FOUNDATION. I'm about to start reading *Is It Me You're Looking For?* Getting set for another revelation – *Grace Sani, Adeyemi College of Education, Ondo, Nigeria*

I've always been a fan of your interesting novels and books right from when I was twelve. Now I'm twenty-four years old and it seems I can't stop marveling at these great books, especially my favorite, *Love Fever*! How I wish I could truly see you one day and hug you because you have really blessed my life through reading your books – *Olufunmilayo Olutimeyin, Ikorodu, Nigeria*

I still have *Love Fever* that I bought since our Secondary School SS1 (2009) and Mrs. Fesobi seized it from someone I lent it to. Then one day after assembly on Saturday, I can't remember what took me to her house, I saw it lying on a table and fiam!, I took my thing back. I remember *Oh Baby*! and *Shadows From the Past* too – *Popoola Esther Morolayo, student, Akure, Nigeria*

You made Secondary School memorable for us. Reading those books was amazing. The librarian banned us from borrowing your books. And when we went to the bookstore at that time, we had read all they had in stock – *Kehinde Owodunni, Owodunni kehinde, Logistics personnel, Lagos, Nigeria*

Even though I have not met you in person, I have been blessed by your spiritual literatures I was privileged to get from my wonderful friend, OrevaOgene. What I read some four / five years ago are now very useful in my ministry. I pray that the inspiration of the Holy Spirit will continue to abide with you – *Ladapo Oluwapelumi Olaniyi, Nigeria*

I'm one of your fans. I bless God for your life. Since I have been reading your books, I'm not the same person again. I have learned to put all my hope in God because I believe that He loves me like *Ufuoma* in *Then Came You. The way you are evangelizing and converting people is unique. Please, where can I get them? – *Disi Eunice Omotayo, Ile Ife, Nigeria*

I almost cried when I couldn't find *With This Ring* because it's my favorite – *Joy IniOluwa Ogunniyi, Student, Ado Ekiti, Nigeria*

You are a wonderful writer. Your books have kept me going since I lost my parents. I started with *This Time Around* which was wonderful. And then *Rape & How to Handle It* , *Shadows From the Past, Love on the Pulpit, Love Fever, Tears on My Pillow, To Love Again, With This Ring, Then Came You*, and now, *The Forever Kind of Love*. You are a blessing to this generation – *Adebisi Rachael Temitayo, Teacher, Ikorodu, Nigeria*

Just finished reading *Then Came You*. I am greatly blessed. The Lord will continue to prosper your ways as you bring happiness and make God's will known to many through your books – *Adebola A. Esther, Business woman, Akute, Lagos, Nigeria*

My first time of reading your books was when I was in Secondary School SS1. Ever since, I fell in love both with you- the author- and your books. Your books are those special ones someone picks to read but finds hard to drop, and one would want to quickly open the next page but at the same time wouldn't want to finish it on time. Each time I get to read your books, I see them as chocolates that I must unwrap carefully and finally devour – *Oluwaseun Ekundayo, Freelance writer, Lagos, Nigeria*

You are God sent to save lives – *Sakeye Olutomi, Ile Ife, Nigeria*

You are one in a million, and a mother to all. You transformed my life with your books – *Kehinde Adedunke Saliu, student, Ogun State*

You're simply a blessing to this generation. I have all your books except *Tears on My Pillow*, and I must say that every one of them has blessed my life – *Grace Oyinloye*

The One For Me had a huge effect on me and made me see things differently – *Olayinka*

I don't know how I feel when reading your books. I'm not yet married but they help me a lot – *Omowunmi*

EXCERPTS

... "So, what about you? Is there a lady here or in Nigeria?" She asked.

He laughed.

She smiled, waiting to hear what he would say.

"Well, if there is, I wouldn't be here alone with you. I would bring her along. There must be commitment and I wouldn't do anything that would make her doubt it." ...

... She added, "My dad will be sixty-nine ... he's six years older than his wife. Er ... when is your birthday?" She returned the phone to him.

"If you're trying to know my age, just ask." He said.

They laughed.

"Not really ... but well, yes, I'm curious about that too." She admitted ...

... They didn't talk for some seconds and then she said, "Er, the other time, I told you that I'm in a relationship,"

He nodded, "Yes you did." *Is she about to reveal the reason she was crying*?

"Well, I just need to make it clear that I'm not looking for another relationship."

The statement took him by surprise, and the bluntness made him laugh. Then he said, "Thanks for making that clear to me but I'm not looking for a relationship either. We're just friends." ...

ACKNOWLEDGMENTS

I thank You Lord for:

Yet another book. Thank You for the privilege and grace You have given me to speak and write for You, and about You - Your will, Your ways, Your word, and Your wondrous love;

My husband, Rev. Sola Odubiyi, and my children, for their love, support, and all that they do for me;

The wonderful people You have blessed me with - my families: the entire Soyombo and Odubiyi families, for always being there for me;

Ojo Olatunbosun and Falola OluwaFeyisetan, who easily accepted to grace the cover of this book with their faces. Falola OluwaFeyisetan does not only believe in this great work, but she has all my books, and sells them. Thank you.

Babatope Olabode who gave up valuable time to edit this book. I appreciate you;

Families, friends, and fans, my avid readers - those who have been with me since the beginning of this great journey, and those who joined along the way, reading my books, supporting, praying, and encouraging me;

I wouldn't have been able to accomplish much without these amazing people You have brought my way. I am grateful, Lord. Let everyone who reads each of these books be blessed, touched and transformed by You. And let them know that You are the real Author, and You're mindful of them!

It's All About You, Jesus!   Taiwo Iredele Odubiyi

DEDICATION

To God

&

To good and godly men, everywhere

# CHAPTER 1

As Dami picked up her black handbag that Saturday evening to leave her bedroom, her phone rang.

It was her friend, Favor. "Hello Dami, where are you?"

"I'm about to leave the house. The mall is just about twenty minutes from my house. What about you?"

"I'm on my way already. I'm on the second bus and will be at the mall soon." Favor didn't have a car and had to ride two buses.

Yesterday, the tenth day of May, was the birthday of one of their friends, Stephanie, and *Steph,* as some people called her, had invited her close friends - Dami, Favor, and Latrisha - to spend some time together this evening, in celebration of her birthday. Dami and the other two ladies had contributed money and bought a gift for her which they would give to her at the mall.

The four single ladies lived in Maryland - a state in the United States of America, met in *Loving God Pentecostal Assembly* where they worshipped, and became close friends. Latrisha was African American while the other ladies were Nigerians.

Stephanie's fiancé, Gabriel, called *Gabe* by friends, had also invited some of his friends to join them. The plan was for them to meet at Lakeworth Mall to watch a Christian movie people had been talking about. It would start at seven-twenty-five in the evening, and then they would go to a restaurant for dinner, afterward.

"Okay then. I'll see you soon." Dami told Favor. "What about the others?"

"You know that Latrisha works in a store by the mall. She has closed at work and is waiting at the mall."

"Okay, I'm on my way." Dami said.

Dami, who would turn twenty seven in January, lived with her much older brother and his family in a single family house, in Maryland. The cozy home located in a quiet area, had a big deck at the back, and the backyard had a private wooden fence.

She graduated from a University in Nigeria where she grew up and her parents and some of her siblings still lived. She relocated four years ago and was now a student in a university while working in a clothing store at Lakeworth Mall.

Her cream-colored room which was in the basement of the house had a twin bed, a closet, a white chair, a trashcan, and a dresser, among other things. The dark brown dresser had a mirror attached to its back, and seven drawers. A pink glass vase with artificial flowers was on a side of the dresser while hair and makeup items took most of the remaining space. A flat screen TV was mounted on a side of the wall.

Standing in front of the dresser now, the dark-complexioned slim lady took a last look at herself in the mirror. She wore a red fitted cotton shirt on black pants, red jewelries, and a two-inch heel black peep toe shoes. The shoes had adjustable sling-back straps.

Her hair was packed in a bun. She used only foundation and powder on her face, and red lipstick on her lips. She could have used more makeup as she sometimes liked to do and fixed her hair for this occasion because Gabe's friends would be there, but she wasn't in the mood. She was going through some stress and would have preferred to stay at home but had to go, to be there for her friend. There was no way she could have stayed away without a reasonable excuse. The four ladies were not only friends, they were also prayer partners.

Still looking in the mirror, she told herself that it would be better she went out than stay at home, feeling upset. She would not go in her car however; she'd ride the bus.

She didn't care what Gabe's friends might think of her simple dressing. She was not likely to see any of them again anyway, she told herself. The three ladies she would meet there were her friends and she didn't need to impress them. Besides, her friends who were Christians like her, knew about the two issues that were causing her stress and had prayed with her. She thought about the issues: a new staff at her workplace had been upsetting her; and Dapo, her fiancé of about a year, had apparently been cheating on her.

She was not supposed to go for this outing alone. Last week, she told Dapo about it and he had agreed to go with her, but only for her to discover the next day that he had not been faithful to their relationship. Since then, he had not contacted her. As she remembered the chats she saw on his phone, she said under her breath, *Lord help me!* She left her room, closing the door gently behind her.

Walking through the mini living room in the basement, she reached the stairway and walked up the stairs. Her brother had taken his four sons out to get their hair cut, and his wife who was at home was not in the main living room.

Dami went in the direction of the Master bedroom and knocked on the door.

"Yes?"

She opened the door gently and poked her head in.

Her sister in-law was in bed, reading a book.

"Aunty, I'm leaving." Dami told her.

She had a good relationship with her brother's wife and had informed the woman earlier that she would be going out to meet her friends. The woman and her family also worshipped at *Loving God Pentecostal Assembly* and she knew Dami's friends.

"Okay. Take care of yourself." The woman said.

Dami left the house, locked the front door with her own key, and checked her phone to know the time. It was six-ten. It was also the second Saturday in May and being summer, the weather had been very warm in the afternoon but now, the sun had gone down, and the heat had reduced.

As she walked down the street, she saw her car - a white Toyota - where she parked it on a side. The bus stop was not far, and when she got there, she glanced at the time on her phone again. It was now six-seventeen, and the bus should arrive soon. A white woman carrying a baby was there and she joined her.

"Hi." She said in greeting.

"Hi." The woman responded with a smile.

A man jogged past them.

Searching inside her handbag, she brought out coins - the exact change for her transport fare. While she waited for the bus, her mind went to her relationship and she began to speak in tongues. Soon, she sighted the bus and moved forward a little. The bus stopped in front of them and the door opened.

The white woman stepped inside with her baby, and Dami followed.

When it was her turn to pay the fare, she greeted the driver. "Hi."

"Hi. How are you doing today?"

"I'm fine, thank you." She answered and paid her fare by dropping the coins in her hand in the machine that collected money.

As she walked over to a seat by a window, her eyes took in the number of passengers. They were about fifteen. She sat down, and the bus pulled away. As it sped off, Dami glanced out the window and continued thinking about her life.

She prayed under her breath, "Lord, defend Your interest in my life. I want to please You, and so I ask You to take control in Jesus' name." Then she started humming a song about God being mighty.

When the bus got close to the mall, she pulled the string near the window to signal her stop. Soon the bus got there, stopped, and six people, including Dami, alighted.

Walking toward one of the entrances of the big mall, she called Stephanie. "I'm here. Where's everyone? Where are we meeting?"

"I'm with the others. We're at the waiting area by the movie theatre. You'll see us."

Soon, she got there and saw her three friends, Gabe, and four of his friends. They were standing together.

"Hi, everyone?" She said brightly. She hugged her friends and then greeted Gabe. "Hi, how are you?"

He returned the greeting and hugged her briefly.

Dami waved at the other men and then looked at Stephanie again. "Happy birthday again."

"Thank you." Stephanie responded. "And thanks for the gift."

It was when Stephanie mentioned the gift that Dami noticed she held a gift bag in her hand. Latrisha and Favor had already presented it to her.

"You're welcome." Dami responded.

"So, er ... let's get to know ourselves." Gabe announced. "Well, I'm Gabriel, and this is my beautiful lady, Steph." He pulled her close.

"Oh, thank you!" Stephanie said and laughed. "*Obrigado*."

Stephanie used the word often and Dami had come to know that it meant thank you in Portuguese.

Dami and the others smiled and teased them.

Gabe looked and pointed at the man standing next to him, and the man, a Latino, introduced himself.

As the men introduced themselves, Dami thought that they must be Christians because Gabe was. They were handsome and jovial but Dami didn't pick their names. She wasn't interested in any of them. She already had a fiancé and what she was interested in was his commitment, so they could get married next year as they had agreed.

"Dami." She said, when it was finally her turn.

Gabe spoke again, "Thanks everyone, for coming. Now, can we proceed?"

"Sure." Some of them said, and they went in the direction of the movie theatre.

At the entrance, each person paid for a ticket, and they went inside. In the lobby, on the way to the movie auditorium, Gabe stopped to buy popcorn for Stephanie.

"Who else is interested?" He asked.

Favor and Latrisha were, but Dami declined.

"Why not?"

She shook her head. "I wouldn't be able to eat dinner."

In the movie auditorium, there were several rows of red padded seats. Taking the side aisle, they all sat on the same row in the middle of the hall, not too close to the screen. Dami had Latrisha on her right, and one of Gabe's friends on her left. When she saw the man shutting off his phone, she did the same. The room was dark, and pictures showed on the large screen on the front wall. Soon, the hall was packed to its full capacity.

At seven-twenty-five, the movie began and everyone was quiet, ready to be taken on an emotional journey. The story was about a couple. The man loved the woman. He defended her and was very committed to her.

As Dami watched it, her mind went to her relationship with Dapo and she told herself – *this is how a good and godly relationship should be. When a man loves a woman and loves God, he will be committed and make the right decisions. He won't do things that will hurt their relationship.* Dapo was supposed to be committed to their relationship and God, after all, he claimed to be a Christian.

She remembered how she checked his phone a week ago when she visited him and saw some intimate chats between him and a lady. Her heart had almost stopped. He broke his promise and broke her heart but rather than apologize, he accused her of not trusting him and intruding into his privacy. For the sake of peace, she apologized for checking his phone, but what about the chats? He denied them but when he realized that she wasn't going to buy his excuses, he got angry.

"I need my space!" He told her.

What did he mean by that? Why would he be asking for space when they were in a relationship and would be getting married soon? At the beginning of their relationship, he didn't care if she checked his phone. He sometimes asked her to answer his calls if he couldn't, but all that had changed, and he now kept his phone in his pocket whenever she was around.

This was the second time he would be cheating on her, or rather, when she would stumble on evidences that he was cheating on her. Last year December, she found his chats with another lady. He denied cheating on her but eventually apologized and promised it would not happen again. He apparently did not mean it. Had there been other women between then and now?

Since last week, he had not contacted her, and she had also not contacted him. She was always quick to call him or apologize whenever they had a misunderstanding, trying to be a good Christian, but she would not contact him this time. He was obviously taking her for granted. He would have to contact her, apologize, and put an end to his wrong ways. When they started the relationship, she discussed with him and they agreed there would be no sex before marriage in accordance with God's word, but it had become obvious to her now that he must have been having his fun outside, even though he used her picture as his WhatsApp display picture, and he was a worker in the church where he worshipped. All of that didn't seem to make much difference to him.

She had been hoping to hear from him since last week but whenever her phone rang or beeped, it was someone else. Didn't he realize he had hurt her? Still, she missed him.

As she thought about her situation with Dapo, tears welled up in her eyes. She didn't deserve his treatment from him. If he decided to end their relationship, where would she start from? She wondered.

Where is he now? Who is he with – the other lady? How serious is the relationship? Is the lady the only one? What should I do? I don't deserve this.

Help me, Lord. I'm Your child, she prayed silently, and tears began to tumble down her face. She quickly dabbed at her face with the back of her hand so that the people on her sides would not see her crying.

CHAPTER 2

Eddie was watching the movie even though this kind of movie wasn't his thing. He found it interesting however, and he was learning some lessons from it.

Then he noticed a little movement beside him. He glanced at the lady and saw her hand go to her face. Was she crying?! Over what?! Why? Was this movie that interesting? Was he missing something?

She might not be crying, he thought, and returned his gaze to the screen but watched her from the corner of his eye. Within seconds, he saw her hand go to both sides of her face again, and even though she tried to hide it, he could see that she was crying. Why? What could have caused it?

Then he heard a sniff.

He looked at her. "Are you okay?" He asked in a whisper.

His deep voice broke apart her thoughts. She nodded and whispered back, "Yes, thank you."

"Do you need something?" He would have mentioned her name, but he couldn't remember it. He hadn't taken note when the ladies were introducing themselves.

"No."

"I have a clean handkerchief ... new actually. Will you like to use it?"

She shook her head. "No, thank you."

He wondered if her friend on the other side realized that she was crying.

Well, he would keep an eye on her. He glanced at her again to take a proper look and saw that she wore a red top. He faced his front, but the movie no longer held his attention. *What's making her cry?*

Dami noticed that he was looking at her, but she ignored him. He should mind his business. When he looked away, she decided to look at him. He wore a shirt ... was that red or brown color? She wasn't sure because of the dimness of the room. She faced her front and tried to focus on the movie. *Dami, pull it together*, she counseled herself.

Soon, the movie ended, and the lights came on again. People began to talk as they moved to the side aisles that led to the exit which was at the back of the room. Their group followed suit.

In the hallway, Eddie looked at her and guessed she was five feet five inches tall. His eyes took in her dressing, starting from her hair. Her fitted red shirt had pointed collar, two fake pockets at chest, and long roll-tab sleeves with button cuffs. He glanced at her bag and shoes, and back up at her face. He noticed that she did not wear a heavy makeup. He liked that. She was simply dressed, yet there was an air of sophistication about her which he thought was beautiful. But why was she crying?

He had told Gabe that he might not go with them for the dinner but as he looked at her, he changed his mind. His friends were Christians and he guessed the ladies were Christians too. Being a member of *The Good Samaritan, and The Follow-up team,* two of the departments in the church where he worshipped, he would like to know why one of Stephanie's friends, a beautiful Christian lady at that - was crying, and if he could help.

****

Dami looked in his direction and saw him looking at her before he looked away. She looked him over as well. His shirt was a burnt orange, worn over jeans. She looked away.

As they walked toward the entrance, she found herself walking beside him. The fairly light-skinned man was tall, and she thought he would be up to six feet. When they neared the door that led to the mall's hallway, he stepped ahead of the group, opened the door, and held it, to allow them pass through.

"Thanks, Eddie." Gabe said.

Eddie's his name. That's short for Edward, she assumed.

She said thank you as she passed him.

At one of the outside doors that led to the parking lot, he came to her and asked, "Did you come in your car or will you need a ride?"

"Oh, er," she looked at Favor.

"Your friends can come if they want." She heard him say, and she told Favor about it.

"Okay, we'll go with him." Favor said.

Dami looked back at him and nodded. "Okay. Thanks."

Outside, Gabe asked, "How are we going?"

"Two of the ladies will go in my car." Eddie said, and pointed at Dami and Favor.

"Victor, you're going with Eddie, right?" Gabe asked one of his friends.

"Yes."

Oh, so another person is going in his car? Better. – Dami thought.

The arrangement was made, and they split up.

"The car is on that side." Eddie told Dami and Favor, and together with Victor, they walked in that direction.

Soon, he pressed a button on the key in his hand and the headlights of a black car flashed. The doors were unlocked and when they reached the car, Dami saw that it was Acura TLX.

The men sat in front, with Eddie behind the wheels while the ladies sat at the back, with Dami behind Eddie.

He started the car and as soon as he pulled out from the space, he spoke, "By the way, I'm Eddie, and this is Victor."

Victor turned to look at them. "It's nice meeting you both."

"I'm Favor."

"And I'm Dami. Thanks for the ride."

"So, did you ladies enjoy the movie?" Eddie asked, and glanced at the rear-view mirror to see Dami's response.

"Oh sure." Favor responded.

"Yes, it was okay." Dami said and nodded.

As they began to talk about it, he intentionally involved Dami in the conversation, and she found herself laughing at some of his funny comments.

When they reached the restaurant, he parked, and Victor phoned Gabe. "We're here."

"We've also arrived. Just getting down from the car."

They alighted and as they walked toward the entrance, they saw the others coming toward them. Again, Eddie held the entrance door open for them and they stepped inside.

Dami glanced around. The restaurant was elegantly decorated and had marble tile floor. There was a waiting area with chairs to sit on while waiting, but the group didn't have to wait. Gabe approached a waiter, spoke with him, and the waiter who wore a white shirt and a multi-colored four-pocket waist apron on black pants, led them to their reserved table. The long rectangular table with four padded chairs on each long side was covered with linen and set with napkins and silverware. A beautiful vase with flowers sat in the center of it while a chandelier hung over it. Soft music played in the background.

"Can we have an extra chair please?" Victor asked the waiter attending to them.

He handed them menus and said, "Sure. I'll be right back." He left.

Eddie sat on a side of the table and Dami found herself on the other side.

"The menu list is impressive." Victor commented, looking at the menu in his hand.

Dami took hers and looked through.

The waiter brought a chair which Gabe put beside Stephanie's, and he sat down.

"Could I get you something to drink first?" The waiter asked nicely.

"Yes, but give us a minute please. We'd like to pray briefly." Gabe said.

"Oh sure. That's okay. I'll be back." The waiter said and left.

The Latino who was called Javier prayed, and they were all chatting and laughing when the waiter returned to take their order. Some minutes after, they began to eat as they continued chatting and laughing.

The conversation drifted to Nigerian schools and when Eddie mentioned the High School he attended in Nigeria, Dami was surprised.

"You went to L.O.H.S.?" Her eyes widened.

"Yes."

"When? Which year?" She wanted to know, looking surprised.

He mentioned the year he graduated, and then asked, "Were you there?" It was now his turn to show surprise.

"Yes. It seemed you were a year my senior." She revealed.

He mentioned the names of some students and she said she knew them.

"Wow!" He exclaimed. "It's indeed a small world!"

"I was a day student. What about you?" She asked.

"I was a boarder." He answered.

Soon, they were all talking about boarding schools in Nigeria and as some of them shared their experiences, Dami laughed.

Eddie said, "I don't really know why my parents thought I needed to be in a boarding school. It wasn't as if I was giving them problems at home. I was young! Some of the seniors were big. When one of them called me and I answered "Sir!" he slapped me on the back and shouted at me, "Who is your father here?! Are you crazy?!" I burst into tears."

They all laughed.

"Are you kidding?" Latrisha couldn't help asking.

"No, I'm serious." Eddie said.

"It's true. Such things happen in some of Nigerian schools." Gabe told Latrisha.

"Oh my God!" She exclaimed.

Eddie went on. "I can laugh about it now but at that time, it wasn't funny. Another time, a senior asked me to fetch water for him, but I forgot. When he found me, he asked me to fetch the water with a spoon to fill a bucket, as punishment."

They laughed again.

Latrisha was also laughing. She almost couldn't believe some of the things she was hearing.

Favor said, "I was also young. When my parents told me they would be taking me to a boarding school, I was excited. They bought different provisions for me, including cans of Geisha,"

"What's that?" Stephanie asked.

"Geisha ... that's mackerel fish in tomato sauce."

"Oh, okay."

Favor continued, "They bought sardine, sugar, milk, and *gari*. I was happy. They followed me to my room but as soon as they left, the seniors who had come to see another senior in my room asked me to open my box. I did, only for them to start taking my provisions one by one. You won't believe they took almost everything! I cried that night until I slept off. In fact, I cried every day for about three weeks."

"I was also in a boarding school." Gabe told them. "And because I was very stubborn, I was always punished by the seniors. There was no kind of punishment I did not serve. I did frog-jump -"

"Oh yeah, I remember that!" Victor said and laughed. "I was also a boarder, but I never did the frog-jump. I was a gentle boy."

"What's frog-jump?" Latrisha asked.

"I was just going to ask the same question." Stephanie said, looking at Gabe. She was three when her family relocated to America and had visited Nigeria only once since then.

Gabe explained. "The person being punished holds both ears and do several squats without stopping. The person would be caned if he stopped."

Stephanie laughed.

"I think I did the frog-jump only once." Eddie said.

"I did it several times." Gabe disclosed.

They laughed.

Gabe went on. "And there was the airplane. The person being punished would stand on a leg and stretch out the second leg and hands, like an airplane in flight, for a long time."

"Oh my God!" Latrisha exclaimed.

"I did that." Favor said.

"I did that a couple of times." Eddie revealed.

"I was small and gentle, so they tended to send me on errands." Victor said. "One day, one of them asked me to fan him to sleep."

"Shouldn't there be some adults to monitor the activities of the students?" Latrisha asked with a frown.

"We had a house master but how could one man effectively manage about one hundred and fifty students; mostly unruly teenagers?" Gabe responded.

"But ... I still don't get it, why do some parents put their children in boarding schools which are usually far away from home when there are good schools around?" Stephanie asked with a frown. "Some children are as young as ten or eleven years old."

"I was ten." Victor stated.

"I was ten plus." Favor told them.

"I was also ten plus." Eddie revealed.

"I knew why my parents sent me to a boarding school. It was because they couldn't handle me." Gabe informed them. "They didn't know what to do with me. I was troublesome."

The others laughed.

Favor said, "I think some of them do it so their children can learn to live independently."

"Yes. I think it's their way of trying to inculcate discipline and responsibility in their children." Eddie commented. "I think they believe that the children will learn these things in the boarding school in a way they may not learn at home. As for me however, I won't put my child in a boarding school in Nigeria. Some of the students are very wicked and have not been taught the fear of God. I won't put my child through those horrific experiences."

Victor too kicked against the idea. "I won't send my child to a boarding school in Nigeria unless I'm certain it's a Christian school that's well managed by godly people with adequate supervision. I don't think I know anyone who went to any of those boarding schools who was not bullied or tormented by some seniors. I almost fainted one day while doing the frog-jump."

"I heard that a boy died after doing it." Dami said. "The so-called senior knew that the boy was tired, but he didn't allow him to stop until the boy collapsed."

"Oh my God!" Stephanie exclaimed. "This is an abuse and it has to stop!"

"I almost went into depression." Favor disclosed. "I don't know how I survived those years. I thought my parents hated me, I mean ... why would they leave me in the hands of such children? Those seniors were simply older children; teenagers who didn't know much. They were children who should still be under the watch of their parents."

Eddie spoke again. "Boarding schools may have some advantages, but I believe that children should be under their parents' watch in their formative years. I'll prefer that my children go to school from home, so that my wife and I can monitor them. God wants us to raise our children for Him. We shouldn't leave the responsibility completely to the school or some teenagers out there with questionable characters."

"That's right!" Stephanie agreed.

Eddie went on. "Should a student in a boarding house copy some bad habits from the peers, such as homosexuality, smoking, drinking; which happens a lot -"

"And there could be sexual abuse and sexual intercourse," Victor chipped in.

Eddie nodded and continued, "The parents might not know on time, but if he or she lives with the parents, they might notice the bad habits at some point and quickly curb them."

Gabe pointed out, "Boarding schools will be okay if there are godly influences and adequate supervision by godly adults, but if those things are lacking, they may do more harm than good."

As the conversation continued, Dami looked in Eddie's direction several times, and some of the times, their eyes met. He was not bad looking, she thought.

When they finished eating, Favor looked at the time and said, "I'll need to leave soon."

Gabe asked Javier if he would be kind enough to drop Favor off at her house and he agreed.

"Tomorrow being Mother's Day, I'll need to get to church very early. My department oversees decoration and refreshments." Stephanie said.

When they were ready to leave, Latrisha was asked to pray and she did. They contributed money to settle the bill that the waiter brought, and then stood to leave.

CHAPTER 3

As they all walked toward the door, Eddie came to Dami. "Do you need a ride home?"

She shook her head. "No, thank you. I'll go with Latrisha."

"Oh, fine. Can I have your phone number?" He had his phone in his hand.

"Sure." She answered and dictated it while he saved it on his phone.

She didn't ask for his because she didn't want to get unnecessarily close to him even though she liked him and liked the attention he was giving her. She didn't want him; she wanted her cheating boyfriend.

"Thank you." He told her.

Outside, she entered Latrisha's car while Eddie and Victor went in the direction of Eddie's car.

Latrisha pulled into the driveway of Dami's house at about eleven. They said goodbye, and the lady drove away. In bed later, Dami prayed, and then thought about the evening. She had enjoyed herself despite the concerns at the back of her mind.

She smiled as she thought about Eddie and how pleasant he was. Was he giving her attention because he saw her crying? If that was it, then she was surprised by both her sudden tears and his sudden attention. He must be a good person. Remembering some of his comments made her smile again.

Or was he interested in her? If he was, then this would be a bigger surprise to her. She wasn't even looking her best. What could he have seen in her?

She was further surprised that they attended the same High School. When did he come to the US? She wondered. *Why didn't I ask for his number? Will he contact me*? She realized she would like to keep in touch with him since they attended the same school. It might come useful later.

Her thoughts soon drifted to Dapo and her heart went into a free fall. *What's he doing? Where's he*?

Her mind went to how they started. They met at a friend's wedding, and she prayed before she agreed to go into a relationship with him. She wanted a man who had a solid relationship with God and who was God's will for her. He seemed so initially, but his behavior since December was becoming confusing to her. *Did I miss it somewhere*?

This was her first serious relationship since she gave her life to Christ at the age of seventeen and she wondered if she was expecting too much from Dapo. She wouldn't want to lose him as he had a lot going for him. However, knowing that God's involvement was important, she prayed again that if he was not the right man for her, or if he would turn her life upside down, God should please separate them!

****

Eddie and Victor shared a two-bedroom luxury apartment, and soon, they were on their way back home. They stopped briefly at Walmart store to buy onion, habanero, and bell pepper which Eddie would need to cook stew the next day.

They got home at eleven-twenty-eight and Eddie parked in his assigned spot, in front of their building. He liked the neighborhood because it was safe, and the apartment center had a swimming pool, a gym, and a playground.

Their apartment was one of the four on the first floor of the building and they had been living there for close to three years. It had a balcony, washer and dryer, and extra storage space.

The tastefully furnished living room was cozy and had a key rack on a side of the wall. Eddie put his bunch of keys on the rack before taking the plastic bag which contained onions and pepper to the kitchen. The clean kitchen had a refrigerator, cabinets, marble counter top, cooker, dish washer, and microwave oven, among other things.

Opening the refrigerator, he deposited the plastic bag in it, and went in the direction of his room. The furniture in the room which had a queen size bed and walk-in closet, included a full-length mirror, a table, a bedside lamp, a cabinet that contained books, and artworks on the cream walls.

Shedding his clothes, he wore pajama shorts, left the room and went into the bathroom for a quick shower. The clean bathroom contained a bathtub with a shower, toilet, and sink. There was a cabinet above the sink with a mirrored door. Other things in the bathroom were towels, a toothbrush holder, a trash can, and shower mat.

Back in his room, he got in bed and thought about the day. He had started it with prayer as he normally did daily. Then he read some chapters of the Bible as he liked to do before getting off bed. The day he couldn't read in the morning for some reasons, he ensured he found time later in the day to read up. He also posted what he tagged *Word for today* on Facebook and Twitter. He started *Word for today* two months ago, posting a verse from the Bible chapters he read in the day.

He later cleaned his room and did a load of laundry before going to the mall to meet his friends. And there, he met Dami. Still surprised that they attended the same school, he checked her phone number on his phone and when he saw her on WhatsApp, he checked her picture. The picture was taken at a beach and she was smiling, with no makeup.

As he looked at it, a smile played on his lips. She was a natural beauty. Unfortunately, he had not been able to find out what made her cry.

Pushing thoughts of her aside, he quickly responded to some chats on his phone. He went on Facebook, saw that some people had responded to his post and he checked the responses. When he was through, he searched for Dami on Facebook and found her easily. He glanced through her posts.

Afterward, he prayed, and prepared to sleep. While he waited for sleep to claim him, he allowed his mind to drift back to Dami. Something about her drew his attention. Was it the way she carried herself, her beauty, or the fact that he saw her crying? Or was God trying to say something to him about her? He was still thinking about her when he eventually slept off.

He woke up at five-thirty on Sunday morning and began to prepare for church service at *God's Heritage Church,* which was about forty-five minutes' drive away. Being church workers, he and Victor must be in church every Sunday morning by seven and attend the two services that would hold, but there would be a combined service today being Mother's Day.

The day's service was wonderful as always, and mothers were celebrated. He and Victor returned home at about one in the afternoon. Victor prepared their tea, adding honey to it, while Eddie prepared omelet which they ate with bread rolls. He went to his room afterward, to rest.

When he woke up at four-thirty, he phoned his mother to wish her a happy Mother's Day, and greeted his father too. Afterward, he returned to the kitchen to prepare stew which he and Victor would eat with rice in the evening. He usually cooked because Victor wasn't a good cook.

He was about slicing some onions when he remembered that the Head of *The Good Samaritan* Department in church asked him to call a woman to find out if she received the foodstuff sent to her by the department. He would phone her as soon as he finished cooking, he told himself.

Later, stretched out on the three-seater sofa in the living room, he took his phone and called the woman. She confirmed that she received the food items and thanked Eddie.

He remembered how the woman was crying the day she approached the church for financial assistance to her family, and his mind went to Dami who was also crying yesterday. He wondered if he should call her to say hello, and to know how she was doing today. Had she gotten over whatever yesterday's issue was? Did she need some form of help? Financial, perhaps?

He looked at the time. It was six-twenty-four. Would she be at home or work? Well, if he called and it wasn't answered, he'd leave a message, he decided.

He called.

****

Dami had made *Ayamase* stew yesterday with which the whole family ate rice when they returned from church at about two-thirty this afternoon. The church service had taken a little longer because of the Mother's Day celebration. The senior pastor of the church also met with the singles executives of which Dami was a member, and he said he'd want the singles to have a special event in June.

Dami had given her sister in-law a gift in church, in celebration of Mother's Day, and now, she took her phone to call her mother. She glanced at the time. It was three-fifty. It would be eight-fifty in the evening, in Nigeria. Her mother would still be awake. Soon, she was talking with her parents and it lasted about thirty minutes.

Afterward, she cleaned her room and the living room in the basement before getting in bed, to take a nap.

Her phone began to ring and seeing an unknown number, she wondered who it was. She answered it. "Hi. Who's this?"

"Dami hi. This is Eddie."

"Oh hi!" She was both surprised and happy to hear from him. Now she could save his phone number. "How are you?"

"I'm doing well. How have you been?"

"I'm good." She said.

"Just thought I should say hi."

"Oh, thank you. I appreciate that."

"Did you go to church today?" He asked.

"Yes, I did. I returned not quite long."

"Where do you worship?"

"*Loving God Pentecostal Assembly*." She answered. "What about you?"

"I attend *God's Heritage Church*."

"Oh, that's Pastor Ola's church. One of my cousins worships there." She said. "I was there when he was getting married. You'll probably know him ... James."

"I know James. He's my HOD, the Head of the Good Samaritan Department. He's your cousin?"

"Yes."

"That's interesting!"

He told her he also belonged to the Follow-up Team in church, and she said she was in Prayer Department and a member of the Singles Fellowship executives.

They talked about their jobs. He mentioned the name of the company he worked for and that he had the privilege of working from home.

"Wow! That's awesome!" She said, and then told him she worked in a clothing retail store at Lakeworth Mall while studying in the University of Maryland. She told him the course she was studying in the University.

"So, how are you today? Is everything okay?"

"Yes, thank you." She answered.

He asked other questions that could make him know what upset her at the movie without being direct, but her answers didn't reveal anything.

When they eventually finished discussing, she told him, "Thanks for calling. I appreciate it."

Afterward, she saved his number, and when she saw the WhatsApp icon, she looked him up.

Looking at his picture, she smiled. It seemed he liked her, she thought, and told herself that if he had crossed her path about a year ago before she met Dapo, she might have considered him, but he came too late. She was already in a relationship and being a Christian, she must be committed to it even if it was giving her stress.

CHAPTER 4

All through the week, Dami was not far from Eddie's thoughts, to his surprise. Did God want him to talk to her again for some reasons? When on Sunday, she was still on his mind, he decided he would phone her again the next day.

****

Dami had just returned home that Monday evening, carrying four bags of groceries into the kitchen when her phone began to ring. Putting the bags on the kitchen counter, she brought out her phone from her handbag.

"Hi." She said and balanced the phone between her ear and shoulder, so she could use both hands to put the groceries in their proper places.

They made some small talks. When she finished in the kitchen, she headed for the basement and heard him ask, "Can we meet again?"

"As in?"

"As in - can I see you again?" He said clearly, sounding amused.

"Er," she thought of what to say. Should she see him? She entered her room, closed the door, and sat on the bed.

When she hesitated, he asked if she'd prefer that her friends were there.

She laughed. "No, I'm an adult."

"So, I'd like to see you again." He was direct.

The bluntness made her smile. "Okay, that's fine. What's the plan?"

"Will you have some time this weekend? Saturday or Sunday?"

"What time on Saturday?" She asked.

"Is the evening okay by you ... probably at seven?"

"Okay, that's fine."

"We can just have dinner somewhere. Would you like me to pick you up?"

"No." She didn't want him to come to her house because her brother and his wife would want to know who he was and ask her questions. Besides, they knew Dapo but didn't know they were having issues and she didn't want them to know ... at least not now.

"Er ... if I know the place, I'd prefer to meet you there." She added, and mentally went through her closet to try to figure out what she would wear. She would dress better this time.

"That's fine. Where do you live so we can find a place that's not too far?"

She told him.

"Oh good." He said and mentioned a restaurant in an area. "Will that work with you?"

"Yes sure. I know the place."

"Great. I'll see you then."

"Yes, bye." She told him.

****

After the call, Eddie phoned Gabe. "How are you?"

"I'm okay. I'm at work."

"Oh, okay."

"What's up?" Gabe wanted to know.

"Well, just a quick one. I got Dami's phone number the other day and I've been in touch with her. Just thought you should know."

"Oh, really?

Eddie chuckled. "Yeah."

"Wow! I didn't even know she captured your attention that day. Do you like her?"

"No, that's not it. What are you talking about?" He immediately replied and laughed. "She -" He was about to reveal that she was crying at the movies but stopped. He didn't think that would be necessary. He said instead, "I just feel like keeping in touch with her. That's all."

"Okay."

When the call ended, he searched the Bible chapters he read earlier in the day and chose a verse to post on social media as *Word for today*. He also posted an inspirational article.

While checking some of his friends' posts on Facebook, he thought about Dami and decided to send a friend request to her. He went on her page, sent the request, and then began to read her posts. The previous day was a shared post.

Jesus must be honored!
As a child of God and a follower of Jesus, don't join the world to write Xmas. It's both intentional and satan's plan to shift focus from Christ and make it an ordinary celebration.

But Jesus Christ is the reason for the celebration. He is the One we celebrate, therefore, be a good example to the world. Write Christmas in full.

And don't write 'ijn' on social media. It should be '"in Jesus' name"'. Jesus is Lord!!!

Also, for God and the Godhead, you should use capital letters.

It must be: God, You, Him, Jesus Christ, Holy Spirit, etc. In this house, pls don't write god, jesus, holy spirit, him, etc.

The first letter should be in capital.

You should also honor God in your marriage, business, everything; doing all to the glory of God.

Let us learn these things and teach them to our children.
Song

🎤 *Jesus must be honored*
Must be honored, must be honored
Jesus must be honored in my life every day.
(By: Pastor Taiwo Iredele Odubiyi)

Hmm, I like this, he thought and shared it on his page.

****

Wondering if she had done the right thing by agreeing to have a dinner with Eddie when she was in a relationship with another man, Dami asked the Holy Spirit to lead her. She thought about it for some minutes and then decided to call him back and cancel the arrangement but just as she was about to take her phone, she felt in her spirit that she should not.

Well, fine. She would meet him, after all, it would be in a restaurant, but she would ensure they kept to neutral conversations.

With that decided, it occurred to her to mention it to Stephanie, and taking her phone, she called her friend.

After the greetings, she said, "How well do you know this guy, Eddie?"

"Eddie? He's Gabe's friend. They've been friends for some time and he knows him well. What happened?"

"Not much. He collected my phone number the other day and called me the next day."

"Wow!"

Dami went on. "He called me again today and invited me to a dinner."

"Really?"

They laughed.

"Eddie is quite fast!" Stephanie commented.

"Fast about what?"

"I didn't know he showed any interest in you on that day, I didn't know anything happened between the two of you."

"Well, it wasn't really like that. Nothing happened. It was just that he happened to be sitting next to me at the movies and saw me crying." Dami informed her.

"You cried?"

"Yes."

"Why?"

Dami hissed. "Don't mind me. I was surprised myself. I just found myself thinking about Dapo, and tears came."

"Wow! So, he saw you crying?"

"I don't know how he knew but yes, he knew. I was surprised when I heard him ask – are you okay? I felt embarrassed." She explained. "I was like – can't a girl cry in peace?"

They laughed.

Dami went on. "That was all. He brought me and Favor to the restaurant, and as we were leaving, he asked for my number."

Stephanie laughed again and said, "You can honor his invitation if you want. He's okay. He's a good Christian."

"I told him yes ... just to see him again, after all we attended the same High School but if he says anything about relationship, I'll let him know that I'm not available."

They eventually said goodnight, and as she was about to end the call, she saw a notification from Facebook on her phone. She checked and saw that it was a friend request from Eddie. She chuckled, accepted his request, and went on his page to know more about him.

She looked at his cover and profile pictures, and then his posts. Today he made two posts, one was an inspirational article, and the other was *Word for today* which was a Bible verse.

Word for today
But Daniel made up his mind that he would not defile (taint, dishonor) himself with the king's finest food or with the wine which the king drank; so, he asked the commander of the officials that he might [be excused so that he would] not defile himself. DANIEL 1:8 AMP

(Don't allow yourself to be defiled.)

Yesterday, the *Word for today* was:

My son, if sinners entice you, do not consent. PROVERBS 1:10 AMP
(Turn your back on them.)

He is definitely a Christian, she thought as she continued scrolling down to see his posts and pictures.

****

On Saturday, Dami dressed well and applied makeup. As an afterthought, she wore false eyelashes which she rarely used, just to appear elegant. She took her car keys and left the house. As she neared the restaurant, she phoned him to know where he was, and he said he was already there.

"I'll be there soon." She told him.

She reached the restaurant at about seven-ten. After parking her car, she slid out of it, and entered the building.

CHAPTER 5

Eddie had been sitting at a table for two, looking toward the entrance, his phone in his hand. The moment Dami walked in through the door, he saw her, and his eyes took in her dressing in one swift look. The long gown she wore was smocked at the waist and ruched at the shoulders. Her jewelries, bag and shoes were silver to complement the elegant gown. Her hair was packed in a bun and she wore makeup.

He stood and came to her, smiling.

She was also looking at him and his smile which she remembered so well, was there. The white shirt he wore on black pants and black shoes, had some embroidery designs at the front, pointed collar, button down front, and two patch pockets at chest.

"Hi." She greeted him and extended her right hand.

He took her hand. "Hi. It's so good to see you again!" He said, with a wide smile on his face.

As they walked over to his table, she could smell his cologne.

He asked, "Did you drive down or did someone drop you off?"

"I drove down. I have a car."

"Oh great!" He said. "And you look great, by the way." The perfume she wore gently teased his nose.

"Thank you. So do you."

They sat down.

"So, how are you?" He asked, smiling as he looked directly into her eyes. He thought that her makeup was too much. Even though it was well done, it made her look different from the lady he saw two weeks ago. If she wore it to impress him, he wasn't impressed. He preferred moderate makeup. *And what's with the false eyelashes?* He rolled his eyes in his mind.

"I'm fine, thank you. The Lord has been good." She answered, looking into his probing eyes. "And you?"

"Great!"

"Eddie is short for Edward, right?" She wanted to know.

"Yes, it is."

They didn't talk for some seconds, and then he spoke again, still smiling. "Gabe said you told Steph that we would meet."

She returned the smile and explained, "Yes, I did ... Steph is my very good friend. You know, I got to know you through her. I didn't want a situation where she would hear about this later and think – *But Dami didn't even tell me that Eddie was getting in touch with her.*"

"That's fine. I understand. I don't have any problem with it. It's the right thing to do. I told Gabe that I'm in touch with you." He flashed her a grin.

They took the leather covered menus on the table, looked through, and decided on what they would eat.

A waiter came and took their order. "And what will you like to drink?"

They both ordered soft drink.

"No ice, please." She added.

"Yes, ma'am." The waiter said and left.

Eddie spoke. "I wasn't supposed to be with you guys that Saturday. I'd planned to visit my parents but on Friday, they called to tell me they would not be available."

"Your parents are here?"

"Yes."

The waiter returned with their drinks.

They thanked him and he left again.

"Where do your parents live?" She asked.

"They're in Virginia."

"Oh, okay. That's nice."

"Let's bless the drink and all that we'll eat." He told her.

He prayed, she said Amen and as they continued talking, they sipped their drinks.

He spoke again. "Are your family members here too?"

"Only my older brother is. The others are back in Nigeria."

"Where's your brother? Is he here in Maryland?"

She nodded. "Yes. I live with him and his family."

"Oh, I see. For how long have you been here?"

"Er ... I've been here for about four years. I came in immediately after my NYSC in Nigeria, that's the mandatory one-year service by Nigerian graduates."

"I know about NYSC, Dami." He said and chuckled.

"Oh yes." She smiled.

"Is Dami short for Damilola?"

"No. My Dami is Oluwadamimoola."

"Oh really? Wow! I'm just hearing the name. I know Oluwadamilola, and Oluwadamilare, but not Oluwadamimoola." He said.

She smiled. "That's what people usually say."

"Er – Oluwadamimoola," He called the name slowly, in a thoughtful manner, and then said, "I guess it means God created me with wealth."

"Correct."

"Oh great! I got it." He said and laughed. "So, where did you serve?"

"I was posted to Kaduna. When did you come here?"

"My family relocated shortly after I graduated from High School." He said.

The waiter returned with the appetizers, *Sesame Chicken Dip*, set them down, and left.

"Thank You, Lord, for this." Eddie said, and they began to eat.

"Hmm, this is delicious." She said.

"It is. How are you getting on at your workplace?"

"I'm okay, I guess." She shrugged.

"Do you go every day?"

"No. I work Monday to Friday. I only go at weekends occasionally."

They continued talking, and then he said, "Can I ask you a question?"

"Sure."

"You don't have to answer though, if you don't want to." A smile tugged at his mouth.

She smiled as she wondered what he wanted to know.

Just then, the waiter brought their main meal, *Chicken and Collards Pilau*. He set it down in front of them and cleared the used plates.

"This looks good." She said, looking at her food.

He nodded.

Taking their cutleries, they began to eat.

"You wanted to ask a question." She reminded him.

"Yes. Er ... I'd like to know, why were you crying at the movie?"

She laughed. "I knew this might come up."

He chuckled as he kept his eyes on her. "I've been wondering about it."

"Well," she thought of what to say, and how much to reveal.

He waited, his eyes searching her face.

"I don't know." She said and shrugged. "I guess I was just feeling a little emotional at that time."

He didn't respond as he waited for her to say more, his eyes probing hers.

She did. "Well, if you must know, I'm in a relationship and ... the movie reminded me of some issues and er -" she stopped, shrugged, and looked at her food.

"Oh, I see."

"But I've prayed about the whole thing." She quickly added. "The Lord is in control."

"Definitely. He is." He agreed. "I guess that the issues are about your relationship. Have they been resolved since then?"

Feeling she had said too much already, she tried to dismiss him by saying, "We're working on them."

"That's good to know. Er ... did you tell him you'd be having dinner with me?"

She took a deep breath and then confessed, "No."

Feeling a need to explain herself so he would not think that she was an unserious Christian or that she was not committed to her relationship, she added, "He's supposed to have called me, but he hasn't. If he had called, I would have told him."

Hmm. "I understand."

She continued, "I tell him everything."

"That's good." He said. "Well, don't fret over your relationship. God watches over His own, I'm sure He will work it out."

"I believe so." She gave a tight smile.

He added, "Jacob didn't think he would see Joseph again, but God made him see not only Joseph but even Joseph's children."

Dami nodded. "That's right."

"He's faithful."

"He is." She agreed with him.

His phone began to ring. He glanced at the screen and said, "Excuse me. I need to take this."

"Go ahead."

The call lasted about a minute. He put the phone down and looked at her.

"So, what about you? Is there a lady here or in Nigeria?" She asked.

He laughed.

She smiled, waiting to hear what he would say.

"Well, if there is, I wouldn't be here alone with you. I would bring her along. There must be commitment and I wouldn't do anything that would make her doubt it."

"That's right. That's how it should be." She said.

She felt like telling him a little more about her relationship with Dapo. She'd also like to ask him some questions, to know if she was the one who was expecting too much from the relationship with Dapo.

I don't really know him, she thought, and changed her mind. She said instead, "I must confess that I'm surprised there's no special lady in your life at the moment."

They laughed.

"Well, it is what it is." He said. "I'm content with my life though. I have to wait until the right lady comes."

He must be around thirty, why is he not in a relationship? she wondered.

They didn't talk for some seconds as they continued eating, and then he spoke again. "I'd like to comment on something."

"What's that?" She smiled, looking at him.

"I hope I won't be misunderstood ... and you can tell me to shut up if you want, I won't feel offended."

What does he want to say this time? She wondered.

"Er ... it's my personal opinion ... and I mean it in a good way."

Her smiled disappeared. *What's this about?*

"I feel that you looked great with your very simple makeup the other day." He said, and quickly added, "As I said, ... it's my personal opinion which I don't think is relevant."

She wasn't sure how to respond immediately as she kept her eyes on him.

"I mean it in a good way."

Wait a minute, what's he trying to say – that I don't look good? "Er,"

"I just thought I should let you know that you're beautiful even without makeup."

She stopped what she was going to say, considered his words, and told him, "Thank you." She was still unsure whether to feel upset, embarrassed, or happy, however.

He hastened to add, "Your makeup is okay ... it was well done, and I think it's sometimes helpful for ladies, but in your case, a little is enough."

She smiled even though she didn't quite get his point. *Where's this going?*

"Let's talk about something else before you tell me to shut up and mind my business." He said and chuckled.

Smiling, she responded, "So, I guess I should assume that you don't really like makeup on a woman."

"Heavy makeup? No." He said frankly. "As I said, makeup is sometimes helpful, to hide blemishes and enhance a woman's beauty. I don't have anything against it, but I think that less is more beautiful in some cases. It's true in your own case."

Her smile broadened.

"Your fiancé must have told you that." He added.

Dapo wanted her to always look beautiful and she used makeup to make him know he had a beautiful woman. However, Eddie was not the first person to tell her that she didn't need heavy makeup. Her brother's wife and a friend in school said the same thing.

"So, when you have a woman, you'll tell her not to use makeup." She wanted to know.

He raised a finger to correct her. "That's not it." He shook his head. "I didn't say no makeup. My 'no' is for heavy makeup. A light makeup is okay, and if a lady needs heavy makeup for some reasons, well, I guess that's okay too. I don't have any problem with that."

She chuckled.

He went on. "And to answer your question, if my woman is using too much makeup, I'll have to have this talk with her. She should be attractive to me. You know what I'm saying?"

She chuckled again and nodded in response to his question.

He smiled and she decided she liked his smile.

"I was in a relationship with a lady sometime ago." He revealed. "She too preferred moderate makeup. I liked it, and complemented her from time to time, to make her know that I was pleased."

Curious, she asked, "Why did the relationship end if you were that pleased with her?"

"A good relationship or marriage takes more than looks."

"Yes, I know." She said. "What happened?"

"Er ... we had different goals."

"Aww." She said. "Can I see her picture?"

He laughed, surprised by the question. "Her picture?"

"Yes. Do you have her picture on your phone or somewhere else?"

"No, I don't. Why would I still have her picture on my phone?"

They laughed.

"I'd have loved to see her picture." She said.

"She's on Facebook."

Smiling, she took her phone and went on Facebook. "What's her name?" She asked, ready to type.

He laughed and told her.

Still smiling, she searched for the name and found her. "Is this the lady?" She turned her phone to him to see.

He nodded.

She looked at her pictures. Yes, the lady was beautiful. "For how long were you together?"

"About six months."

"Wow!" She exclaimed. "What a pity."

He shook his head. "We know that all things work together for the good of those who love God." He stopped. He hoped she knew the scripture he'd just quoted.

She did and showed it by completing the scripture. "Those who love God and are called according to His purpose." She nodded. "You're right."

"God has good plans for His children." He added. "I'm glad He made me stop the relationship on time."

She nodded thoughtfully, and then put the phone down. "So, you deleted her pictures when the relationship ended?

"Umm hmm," He nodded. "I had to. I didn't need to keep them again."

Her phone rang. It was Latrisha. She'd call her later, she thought, and ended the call.

"You can answer it."

"It's Latrisha. I'll call her later." She said.

"Okay."

She spoke again. "So, do you and ... what's the name of the lady?"

"Jiru?"

"Jiru? Is she a Nigerian?"

"Yeah."

"So, do you and Jiru talk sometimes?"

"Not really. We exchange greetings and prayers on birthdays and festive periods. That's all." He said, and then added, "There was a time she needed my help for her younger brother, and she called me. Other than that, there's nothing."

"So, did you end the relationship, or she did?"

"We both did. We met to discuss, and we both agreed that it was best that we ended the relationship." He revealed.

The waiter returned with their desserts and removed the used plates.

Eddie and Dami discussed the Bible and continued talking until they finished eating.

She eventually consulted her phone to know the time. It was nine-ten. "I need to leave soon."

He signaled at the waiter and the bill was brought.

While he settled the bill, her phone alerted her of a message and she checked it. It was from Stephanie.

Are you back at home? How did it go?

Smiling, she responded.

About to leave. Talk to you later.

Outside, he walked her to her car and waited for her to start it. As she pulled away, he waved and said, "See you some other time."

"Alright. Take care." She responded and returned the wave.

He turned and strode to his car.

 CHAPTER 6

On the way home, Eddie filled Dami's thoughts. She liked him and liked the fact that he seemed sincere and open. She almost couldn't believe that he wasn't in a relationship with any lady; being handsome, caring, intelligent, and a Christian. Any lady would be glad to be attached to him.

Remembering some of his words, she wondered if he invited her to the dinner to get to know her better, or if it was because he wanted to know why she was crying at the movie.

Well, she might not know what to think, but she knew what to do. If he made it clear at any time that he'd want to be more than a friend, she'd cut him off. She already had Dapo, and as she had told Eddie, they were working on resolving their issues. She was praying for Dapo to be all that she wanted him to be.

But am I still in a relationship with Dapo? Do I still have him? Can we overcome these issues? The questions rushed at her, and she began to pray about him again. She counseled herself to remain committed to her relationship with him and reach out to him if she didn't hear from him by Tuesday.

She returned home at nine-forty-eight, and shortly after, she received Eddie's call. "Are you back at home?" He asked.

"Yes, thank you." She said. "And thanks for the dinner. I had a good time."

"The pleasure was mine."

"Are you at home too?"

"Yes."

After the call, she phoned Stephanie and told her about the outing.

In church the next day, it was announced that there would be a special singles program on the last Saturday in June, and the singles were expected to invite their friends.

After the service, the singles had a brief meeting, to begin to plan for the event. It was decided that Dami would give a five to ten minutes word of exhortation on that day, Stephanie and three other ladies would oversee refreshments, while Latrisha and a man would anchor the event. One of the men would take the opening prayer while Favor would take the closing prayer. Some other people would handle other aspects of the event.

After the meeting, Dami and her three friends met for prayers as they usually did twice a month, to pray for one another. When it was her turn to be prayed for, they prayed about her relationship with Dapo, and that God's will would be done.

The prayers lasted about twenty minutes, and as they walked to the car park afterward, Latrisha said, "Dami, I called you yesterday evening, but it seemed you ended the call."

"Oh yes, I'm sorry. I was going to call you back when I got home but I forgot. I was with Eddie."

"Eddie?!" Favor stopped walking, apparently surprised.

Stephanie and Dami burst into laughter.

They stood on a side to talk.

"Who is Eddie?" Latrisha wanted to know.

"He's one of Gabe's friends who came for my birthday celebration." Stephanie explained.

"Wow!" Latrisha exclaimed.

Smiling, Favor asked, "Why were you with him?"

"We went out for dinner."

"What?!" Favor and Latrisha expressed surprise again.

Laughing, Stephanie said, "I was also surprised when she told me that he asked her out."

"But ... I was in his car with you. When did you guys exchange numbers?" Favor asked.

"Okay, spill it out, Dami." Latrisha said. "What's going on?"

Dami laughed and said, "Nothing is going on." She told them how Eddie noticed that she was crying at the movie, asked for her phone number, and invited her to dinner.

"Wow!" Latrisha and Favor exclaimed again.

"So how was the date?" Latrisha asked.

"It wasn't a date." Dami denied.

"Whatever." Latrisha dismissed. "How was it?"

"I think he just wanted to know why I was crying." Dami said and rolled her eyes.

"You can roll your eyes all you want, that was a date." Stephanie told her.

Dami laughed.

"The way you're laughing shows that you must have had a good time." Favor pointed out.

"What are you talking about?" Dami asked in mock anger.

"No, the question is, what did you talk about, with him?" Latrisha said.

Dami told them how the dinner went and when she mentioned his comment about heavy makeup, they laughed.

Latrisha spoke again. "We're praying for you about your relationship with Dapo. God's desire will be done. If he's the right one for you, he will change and stay with you, but if he's not, God will remove him and bring the right man into your life."

The others said Amen.

"Have you heard from him?" Favor wanted to know.

Dami shook her head. "No."

"Something is wrong with this relationship." Favor said.

"Some things are wrong with the relationship." Stephanie corrected her. "I really don't know why you're still with him."

"That's why we're praying for her." Latrisha said. "Let's keep praying."

"God can change him." Dami said. "That's what I'm trusting God for."

"God can change him but is he willing to change?" Stephanie asked.

Dami took a deep breath. "I think I'll call him if I don't hear from him by Tuesday."

"Why do you want to call him?" Stephanie wanted to know.

"So that we can talk." Dami answered. "Or do you think I should tell one of his friends about it?"

"You know we want the best for you but if you're not yet married and these things are happening, then I think there's a problem." Favor said.

"If you have to involve his friend to talk to him before he would do the right thing, then I don't think he's the right one for you." Stephanie said. "He's supposed to be committed to your relationship. Simple. The issue shouldn't take this long to resolve."

Favor added, "You're not yet married and he's already a prayer point for you, that's not a good thing."

Dami took a deep breath. *They are right. What's the way forward?*

In the evening, Dapo phoned her. Happy and surprised, she picked it up immediately but controlled her voice so she would not appear excited.

"How are you?" He asked in a dry tone.

"I'm fine. And you?"

"Fine. How's work?"

"Work is fine." She answered. "And how's work at your end?"

"It's okay."

They didn't say much and when she realized he was about to end the call, she said, "Dapo, we need to talk."

"What about?"

"Everything." She said. "I'm surprised you asked that question. Don't you think we need to talk?"

"We've already talked. We've said all that needed to be said on that particular matter." He told her firmly.

"Yes, but nothing has been resolved." She said in a pleading voice. "We haven't talked since then. You didn't call me, you -"

"I didn't call because you upset me."

"What did I do to upset you? What did I do wrong?" She asked. "You're the one who did the wrong thing, you're the one who -"

"There we go again!" He stopped her. "What did I do wrong? Yes, you saw my chats with the lady, but I told you that they're not the way they seemed!"

"How can you tell me that? You're in a relationship with me but telling another lady that you love her, does that seem right to you?"

"I told you that I didn't mean it in the sense of real love. I used the word *love* the way a brother would mean it for his younger sister." He said.

"Is she your younger sister?" She was beginning to feel upset again.

"No, but the Bible talks about loving everyone." He said.

"And that's why you're telling her that you love her?! Dapo, do you think I'm a child?!" She was upset now. "You were with her two days before then, and you said you'd like to see her again. She immediately sent her picture to you in which she was half nude, almost naked. You responded with a smiling emoji and said, *Oh my God.* Is that the kind of love the Bible talks about?"

"Look, the girl was very playful, and I was just playing along." He laughed in a way that said he found her accusations ridiculous.

"Don't insult my intelligence, Dapo!" She said angrily.

"There's nothing between me and her, Dami. I'm a Christian! I'm a worker in my church!"

"Exactly why I'm concerned. This sort of thing shouldn't continue. It shouldn't have happened in the first place. The people of the world may do them but those who claim to know God should not!" She pointed out.

"I've already told you there's nothing between me and the lady but if you don't believe me, there's nothing more I can do about it."

"I don't believe you because this has happened before. It's not the first time, and it's wrong." She said. "You promised me then that it would not happen again."

"Look, you were not supposed to have checked my phone in the first place. If you had trusted me, you would not have checked my phone, but you clearly don't."

"If I checked your phone but didn't see the picture and chats, did you realize that we would not be having this conversation now?"

He was quiet.

When he didn't respond, she spoke again, "We're getting married, Dapo. There must be commitment, don't you understand?"

"I don't think you want to marry me." He said coldly.

"Of course, I want to."

"No, I don't think so." He countered. "Or maybe I should say that I can't marry a lady who doesn't trust me."

What's he talking about? Is he trying to end our relationship? She wondered, half afraid. "Look, we can't discuss this on phone. When can we meet to talk?"

"I don't know."

"You don't know? Can't you come in the evening when you close at work, probably tomorrow or on Tuesday?!" She asked.

"I'm not sure. I'm a little busy at work now."

She took a deep breath.

"I'll let you know when I'll come. I'll find time." He said, not committing himself.

"Okay." She didn't know what else to say.

"Okay, bye."

"Bye."

As she put the phone down, she held her head, feeling very upset. *What's going to happen to our relationship and plans? Everyone close to me knows that I'm in a relationship with him. Should he decide to end the relationship, what would I do? I'll be twenty-seven soon!*

She began to cry as she wondered - is it normal for men to cheat on their women? Should I push my opinions aside and overlook the issue?

She considered the questions and answered no to both. *It's not normal, and there are men who would not cheat no matter the temptation. What people do is a matter of who they are.*

Another question occurred to her – should she agree to have sex with him so he would not have to look for fun outside, that way, she would be able to keep him? *No, no, I can't do that. It's a sin, and two wrongs don't make a right*, she quickly told herself.

She was still crying and thinking when her phone notified her of a WhatsApp chat. She took it and when she saw that the chat was from Eddie, she put the phone down without checking it.

When she felt better some minutes after, she took the phone, opened Eddie's chat, and read.

Word for today
Why are you in despair, O my soul? And why have you become restless and disturbed within me? Hope in God and wait expectantly for Him, for I shall again praise Him For the help of His presence. PSALMS 42:5 AMP.

Hmm, she took a deep breath. Feeling that God made Eddie send the verse to her at this time, to talk to her, she read the verse again, and again. *What is God saying?*

As she read it the fourth time, the answer came to her spirit. *God wants to know why I'm feeling troubled and disturbed when I have Him and He's on the throne. He's reminding me to hope and rest in Him, and I'll have a testimony.*

She began to talk to God. *Thank You for sending Your word to me and being mindful of me, but if I will have a testimony eventually, how do You intend to work things out?*

She kept quiet for some time, to hear what the Holy Spirit would say to her but the only thing she seemed to hear was that she should trust God.

When she finished praying, she sent a message to Eddie.
Thank you. The verse spoke volumes to me; it came at the right time. Have a blessed night.

She received his reply.

Glad to know that it ministered to you. Goodnight.

Favor phoned her in the evening of the next day and in the course of their discussion, Dami told her that Dapo called her last night.

Favor commented, "I really don't know why a Christian man would cheat. It's so annoying. My dad cheated on my mom and I know how upset she was."

"Really? And what did she do?" Dami wanted to know. "They're still together, right? She stayed with him?"

"Yes." Favor answered. "He confessed and stopped seeing the other lady, but the whole trouble could have been avoided in the first instance."

"Hmm, I guess I have to keep forgiving Dapo." Dami said.

"No, that's not the point, Dami. The cases are not the same." Favor told her. "In my parents' case, the infidelity happened inside their marriage. My dad confessed and stopped. In your case, you're not yet married. This is the second time it's happened within months, and it doesn't seem like he realizes it's wrong. You should forgive him, but you also need to let God speak to you concerning the relationship."

After the call, she prayed and told God she was leaving everything about her relationship in His hands.

 # CHAPTER 7

Eddie phoned Dami on Friday which was the last day of May.

"Happy last day of the month." He said.

"Thank you. Wish you the same."

They talked for some time and when he told her that he had vigil in church in the evening, she said she had vigil too.

The next day, first of June, he sent a message to her.

In this new month, you will have testimonies to share, in Jesus' name.

She responded.

Amen. And I pray that the Lord will perfect all that concerns you in Jesus' name. Happy new month.

Amen. Thanks. Have a great day.

On Thursday evening, she decided to call him. "I just thought that I should say hello. How have you been?"

They ended up talking and laughing for about forty minutes.

On Saturday afternoon, she received the flier of the singles event on WhatsApp, and when she wondered who she could invite, the first person that came to her mind was Eddie, but would he be able to attend? She would have to call him today or tomorrow to invite him, she thought.

She was happy when he phoned her in the evening. After exchanging pleasantries, she said, "I was thinking of calling you this afternoon."

"Really? What's up?"

"I'd like to invite you to a special Singles event in my church. It's towards the end of this month, the last Saturday, at four in the afternoon."

He laughed. "This is interesting. I also wanted to invite you to an event in my church, that's why I called."

She laughed. "I hope it's not on the same day."

"I don't think so. This is on the twenty third of June. It's a Sunday, at six in the evening."

"Alright. I should be able to attend. I don't think I have anything slated for that evening. You can send the details to my phone." She said.

"We have invitation cards. I'll be coming to the mall on Tuesday to get something. I'll bring a card for you. Will you be working on that day?"

"Yes." She answered.

"Okay. I'll see you then."

"Er ... should I send the details of my church's event to your phone?" She wanted to know.

"Yes, sure. I'll try to be there."

"Thanks."

After the call, she forwarded the flier with the details of the event to him on WhatsApp.

About a minute after, her phone alerted her of a message. It was from him.

Received. Will be there by God's grace!

She replied.

Thanks. See you on Tuesday

She felt she should invite Dapo to the event as well, but instead of calling him, she sent a message on WhatsApp.

She received his reply about ten minutes after.

Don't think I'll be able to attend. Have to be somewhere.

Well, she had done her part. She remembered she had not prepared the message she would share at the upcoming singles' event and setting her phone aside, she prayed that the Holy Spirit would guide her. She eventually chose the topic *Be an Example*, and her text would be: *Let no one despise your youth, but be an example to the believers in word, in conduct, in love, in spirit, in faith, in purity. (I Timothy 4:12 NKJV)*

After service in the church the next day, Dami and her friends began to discuss the singles' event. Favor said she had invited two friends, and Stephanie said Gabe would be coming.

Dami revealed that she had invited Eddie and she would be going to his church for an event in two weeks' time.

"Seems you guys have become really good friends." Favor teased her.

Dami laughed, and then asked if any of them would be available to attend Eddie's event with her so she would not be alone.

Latrisha eventually agreed to accompany her.

On Tuesday, Eddie came to Dami's store at about three in the afternoon and saw her attending to a customer.

"Hi."

"Hi." She responded, happy to see him.

Realizing that the customer would soon leave, he stood on a side, to wait for Dami. He liked the white sweater she wore on jeans.

Soon, she was through with the customer and the man left. She turned to Eddie, smiling broadly. "Good to see you." She was surprised at the excitement she felt.

"Same here. Are you doing well?"

"Sure." She answered.

Two teenagers entered the store.

"Hi." She greeted them and then faced Eddie again.

"Well, I can see you're busy. I need to get one or two things. I'll look around to see what you have here."

"That's good. Feel free ... and if you need assistance, let me know."

"I will, thanks." He said and left.

Soon, she saw him coming, holding some clothes.

"Are you taking those?" She asked.

"Yes. I like them."

"I'm happy to hear that." She looked at the clothes. "Those are good colors you picked."

She went to the payment register, he paid, and as she folded the clothes, putting them in the store bag, she asked, "Where's the invitation card?"

"It's with me. I'm still in the mall to get some other things. I'll hang around till you close."

She handed the bag to him and as he headed for the door, she looked at him.

When she closed at work, she left the store, and headed for the restroom to freshen up. There, she stood in front of the mirror and looked at herself. Her hair was okay. She applied powder to her face, lip gloss to her lips, and taking her perfume, she sprayed a little. Good.

She washed her hands, dried them under the hand dryer, and left.

Standing on a side in the hallway, she phoned him, "I've closed. Where are you?"

He said he was inside a store. "I'm about to pay. I'll be out soon."

"Okay, you'll find me in front of JCPenney."

There was a bench there and she sat down beside the white man sitting on a side. She greeted him, leaned back, and looked as people walked past. Soon, she saw him coming, holding three plastic bags.

She stood.

"I used the opportunity of being here to get a Father's Day gift for my dad." He explained when he reached her.

"Oh yeah. That's on Sunday. I'll have to get something for my brother too."

"Can I buy you something to eat at the food court?" He asked.

She stared at him for some seconds, and then consulted her wristwatch before she nodded. "Okay, thank you." She was hungry.

As they went in the direction, she said, "I'm wondering what to buy for my brother. He seems to have everything. I think he has enough clothes, belts, and shoes. Even wristwatches."

"In that case, why don't you give him a gift card? He can buy whatever he wants with it." He suggested.

"You're right. Okay."

"My father mentioned to me at a time that he liked a particular thing, and that's what I went to that store to buy." He revealed.

At the food court, they went to Burger King, and he bought Whoppers and drinks for them. Carrying their trays, they went to a table and sat down.

"Thanks." She said again.

"You're welcome."

He brought out the gift for his dad and showed her. He said, "I will mail it to him tomorrow so it can be delivered to him by Saturday."

"It's nice." She said, checking it. Then she asked, "How many siblings do you have?"

"Just one, a female. How many do you have?"

She returned the gift to him and said, "I have three, and they're older. I'm the youngest."

He smiled. "So, you're the baby of the house."

"You can say that again. My conception was a surprise for my parents, they thought they had stopped having children."

They laughed.

"My immediate older sibling is seven years older than I, and whenever my siblings tease me about being a surprise child, I tell them that our parents saved the best for last."

He laughed again and said, "That's a good one."

There was silence for some seconds.

He spoke again. "My sister's getting married sometime next year."

"That's wonderful. Is the man a Nigerian?"

"No, he's White."

She smiled. "How do your parents feel about that?"

"They're okay with it. The guy is a Christian, born again, and that's what matters to them."

"Your parents are born again too?"

He nodded. "Yes. They're ministers in the church they attend."

"Is your sister in Virginia with them?"

"No, she's in California."

"Wow! That's some distance away." She said and smiled.

"It is."

"I was there last year for my aunt's eightieth birthday."

"Eightieth?!" He exclaimed. "That's awesome."

"It is. She's blessed." She said. "It was an elaborate ceremony."

"It should be. Old age is a blessing. My parents are sixty-one, and sixty-three."

"Your mom is sixty-one?"

"No, she's sixty-three."

"Your dad is sixty-one?" She asked, surprised.

"Yes." He chuckled. "He's two years younger than her."

"Wow!" She laughed. "It really doesn't matter anyway."

"It doesn't matter to them. Surprisingly, he looks older than her." He said, smiling. "Er, let me see if I have any of their pictures on my phone."

He began to search, swiping his phone. Then he said, "Okay, I have one here."

He clicked on the picture, enlarged it, and gave his phone to her.

As she looked at the picture, he studied her face.

"Wow, she looks good for sixty-three." She said, smiling. "My mom is the same age as her, sixty-three."

"That's good."

She added, "My dad will be sixty-nine ... he's six years older than his wife. Er ... when is your birthday?" She returned the phone to him.

"If you're trying to know my age, just ask." He said.

They laughed.

"Not really ... but well, yes, I'm curious about that too." She admitted.

"I'll be twenty-nine in February .... second of February precisely."

"Oh, okay."

"What about you?" He asked. "Although my guess is that you're around twenty-six."

"You're close. I'll be twenty-seven in January."

He eventually brought out the invitation card from his shirt pocket and placed it on the table, in front of her.

Taking it, she looked at it. "Okay, I'll try to attend."

"Thanks."

"Oh, and Latrisha will be there too. Do I need another IV for her?"

"Not necessarily but I can give you." He said and brought out another card.

"Thanks."

They didn't talk for some seconds and then she said, "Er, the other time, I told you that I'm in a relationship,"

He nodded, "Yes you did." *Is she about to reveal the reason she was crying*?

"Well, I just need to make it clear that I'm not looking for another relationship."

The statement took him by surprise, and the bluntness made him laugh. Then he said, "Thanks for making that clear to me but I'm not looking for a relationship either. We're just friends."

She chuckled. "I just wanted to be upfront. I hope I didn't embarrass you."

He laughed again. "No, it's okay. That's fine. Maybe I should say that I'm not looking for a relationship with you but I'm trusting God for one."

She smiled.

He spoke again. "Look, this was what happened,"

She listened.

"On that Saturday, I kept wondering why you were crying and when you said you attended my school, I thought I'd like to get to know you better, that's all. Does that put your mind at rest concerning my intentions?"

She smiled. "My mind was at rest. I just wanted us to be on the same page."

"Good. Now that you mentioned your relationship, how has it been? Has he called you since then?"

"Yes."

He noticed that she suddenly looked sad. He stared at her, hoping she'd say more. When she didn't, he asked, "Is everything okay now? Are you okay?"

"Yes."

"Have you settled the issues?" He asked, his voice gentle. His guess was that the issues had not been resolved.

"Not really." She lowered her gaze. "We're still trying to resolve them."

His guess was right. He told her, "I think it's taking too long. Why don't you involve someone for counseling if you can't resolve them on your own?"

She didn't talk.

He spoke again. "And if you'd like to use me as a sounding board, I'm available." He hoped she'd trust him enough to reveal whatever the issues were.

"Well, not as a sounding board per se," she said and looked into his curious eyes. "But since you're a Christian, a man, and ... a friend, I'd like to get your opinion on some things."

"Okay." He concentrated on her face. "I'm a good listener. I won't share what you tell me with people."

"Thanks. If you're in a relationship with a lady, would you tell another lady *I love you?*"

"*I love you?*" He repeated with a frown as if to say *Why would I do that? That's stupid.* "No."

"Would you be visiting another lady or tell her you need her this night?"

"No!" He said firmly.

"What would your reaction be if this lady sent a nude picture to you?"

"A nude picture?"

She nodded.

"Personally, I don't tolerate such things. I would be angry, warn her never to send such to me again, and I'd most likely block her on my phone. However, I don't think a lady would send a nude picture to a man unless there's some kind of closeness or relationship between them."

She didn't talk again.

"Were these what happened?" He leaned forward.

She sighed, nodded, and said, "This is the second time this is happening. It happened in December."

"The same lady?"

"No, that was another lady. When I stumbled on his intimate chats with the first lady, he denied the whole thing for some time but eventually apologized. But this time, he's angry. I apologized for checking his phone but he's not apologizing for the chats. He said he was only playing with the lady."

"Wha-t?!"

She nodded. "Umm hmm."

"What was his response to the nude picture?"

"He sent a smiling emoji and said *Oh my God.*"

"What?" He exclaimed and frowned.

She went on. "He said he was just being friendly with her and that I should trust him. I told him he needed to apologize, confess, and repent but he has refused. Am I wrong? Am I asking for too much? Am I reading too much meaning to the chats?"

"You're not asking for too much, and the chats are clear enough. I'm not going to talk about him because I don't know him, but I will talk about the conduct of a true Christian man. A true Christian man would not put himself in such a situation in the first place. And if he received a nude picture from a lady, he would scold her and warn her never to repeat it. Well, that's what I would do."

"He didn't do any of those."

"If a man who claims to be a Christian is having such chats with a lady, then he's very wrong. I think you should involve someone, probably a pastor." He suggested.

"Dapo won't like it ... I'm not sure he will see the person."

"So, what will you do?" He asked.

"I'll just continue praying until something happens or I know what to do." She said.

She thanked him for the refreshment and for listening to her.

On her way home the next day, she bought a $100 gift card for her brother. Putting it in a small white envelope, she kept it in the handbag she would take to church on Sunday.

That Sunday morning, she went to church with her brother's family. The service went well and when it was time to appreciate fathers, she went to her brother who was with his family. She wished him a happy Father's Day and gave him the envelope. After the service, she gave Latrisha the card for the event in Eddie's church, and at home, she phoned her father in Nigeria to appreciate his role in her life.

# CHAPTER 8

The following Sunday, Dami was back in church. She and Latrisha talked and agreed to meet in Eddie's church in the evening.

After lunch at home, she rested and got up at about four to begin to prepare. When she wanted to use makeup, she remembered Eddie's comment about heavy makeup. *Well, he's not my fiancé, and I don't need to please him*, she thought and continued what she was doing.

The praise and worship had started when she got to the church. She reserved the seat beside her for Latrisha and when the lady arrived shortly after, she came over. After the service, Eddie came to them and thanked them for honoring his invitation.

"We were blessed." They told him.

****

As they talked, Eddie noticed Dami's heavy makeup but didn't talk. He should not make it his business, it wasn't as if they were in a relationship, he told himself.

"I'll see you on Saturday." He told them when they were leaving.

Shortly after he returned home, he received a call from Gabe.

"I'm sorry I couldn't attend the event." Gabe said.

"That's okay. I understand."

"Did Dami come?"

"Yes, she came with Latrisha."

"Steph said you've been invited to the event in their church. Will you be there?" Gabe asked.

"Yes."

"Okay. I'll see you there, then."

Eddie phoned Dami on Tuesday evening. They talked about different things and when the talk got to her relationship with Dapo, he said, "I'm all ears if you'd like to talk a little more."

"He said he wants some space and we haven't talked much since then. I haven't even seen him."

Eddie shared his opinion with her, "A person who has been hooked cannot be asking for space. Marriage is being bound to the spouse, thereby giving up your space. If he's asking for space ... whatever that is, then he's not ready for marriage."

As he thought about Dami later, he remembered the advice he gave her. He knew it was the right counsel, but he also knew that if Dapo and Dami resolved their differences, and everything was fine between them, he would have to pull back from Dami. They could not remain close friends unless Dapo was a part of the friendship.

Thinking about it, he realized that he wouldn't want to lose his friendship with Dami. He liked her and liked her spirit. The only thing he could say he didn't like was her heavy makeup.

****

While Dami went about her everyday normal routine that week, Eddie was not far from her mind and she found herself looking forward to his calls. He was a good man and knowing she would be seeing him again on Saturday made her happy. She couldn't help wondering if he liked her as a woman. Was something developing between them? He had said he and Jiru parted ways because they had different goals, but could she and he have same goals?

On Saturday morning, he phoned her to know the time she would be in church.

"I asked because I'll be coming from my office and would like to come straight to your church rather than go home first." He explained.

"I'll be there by two-thirty." She said. "I have to be there early because I'm an executive member."

"Alright."

When she revealed that she would give a brief word of exhortation, he said he'd love to listen to her.

At about one in the afternoon, she began to prepare, and soon, she wore a gown she bought recently. She didn't use much makeup because she wanted to please Eddie. Somehow, his opinion was beginning to matter to her.

By two-thirty, she was in church and she headed for the event hall which was beside the church auditorium. Round tables and chairs had been covered with red linen and arranged in the fairly large hall.

Favor and Dami chose one of the tables for six, and reserved the remaining four seats for Gabe, Eddie, and the two people Favor had invited, none of whom had come. Stephanie was in the kitchen while Latrisha was talking with some people.

"Is that not Eddie?" Favor asked Dami, looking toward the door.

Dami looked in the direction and when she saw him, her heart began to race. "Yes, it's he." She checked the time. It was three-thirty-five. He had said he'd come early.

She stood, went to him and welcomed him. As he walked beside her to her table, she felt proud to be seen with him. It was as if they were a couple.

He sat beside her and she said, "I thought you might come with Gabe."

"No, we didn't plan to come together, but he phoned me just as I was getting ready to leave my house that he wouldn't be able to attend."

"Really? I'm not sure Stephanie is aware."

"He must have told her." He said. "You can mention it to her, however."

"I will."

He spoke again. "I may need to leave immediately after the sermon. I have a deadline to meet."

"Okay."

****

Eddie glanced around the well-decorated hall, taking in his surroundings. Soon, his eyes returned to Dami and seeing that she wasn't looking in his direction, he stared at her. Her face was just a few inches away and he noticed that her makeup was moderate.

He liked what he saw and taking his phone, he clicked on camera, and called her. He aimed the phone at her and said, "Move close to Favor, so I can take your pictures."

Smiling, she told Favor about it.

"Oh, okay." Favor liked the idea.

They posed and he took a few shots.

"Will you send them to us?" Dami asked him.

"Yes, sure. Right away." He said. "I'll send them to you and you can forward them to Favor."

Soon, she received them on her phone, and she forwarded them to Favor.

She suddenly turned to him again and caught him looking at her.

Not sure what to say, he smiled.

She returned the smile and said, "I need to see Steph. Give me some minutes please."

She stood.

****

In the kitchen, Stephanie and the people in charge of refreshments were busy. A projector screen hung on the front wall of the room that enabled them to see all the activities inside the hall.

Dami told Stephanie that Gabe would not be coming.

"Really?" Stephanie took her phone to call him and found some missed calls and a message. "Oh wow, he's been trying to reach me!"

Dami also told her that Eddie would not wait till the end of the event when refreshments would be served.

"When he's ready to leave, let me know and I'll give you some things for him." Stephanie said.

When Dami returned to the hall, she saw that the man who would take the opening prayer was already standing in front and had asked everyone to stand for prayer. She came to the table and took her place, in between Eddie and Favor.

When the prayer ended, the man put the mic down, left, and a group of four people replaced him. Soon, the hall was filled with music as the congregation praised and worshipped God. The praise and worship session was followed by the welcome address delivered by the President of the Singles Fellowship, a special song by a lady, and then it was time for Dami's talk.

Taking her phone and small jotter, she stood and went to the front as people clapped. She began with prayer, and then acknowledged her audience.

Eddie used his phone to take some pictures of her, and when she began to deliver her message, he put the phone down and listened with rapt attention. He was impressed.

When she returned to her seat beside him, he showed her the pictures.

"Oh, they're great! Thank you."

"I'll forward them to you now."

He did, and she thanked him again.

The event progressed, and when he was ready to leave at six-thirty, she got up to see him off. At the door, she asked him to wait so she could collect snacks and a can of juice for him, but he said it wasn't necessary.

She wouldn't hear of it though. "Give me a few minutes please."

She quickly left and went to the kitchen. Stephanie had packed two bags containing snacks and bottles of soft drinks, and she handed them over to Dami.

"For Eddie and Victor."

"Thanks." Dami said, returned to Eddie, and gave the two plastic bags to him. She saw him off to his car and waited until he slid inside.

He called her later in the evening, at a little past nine, and she soon found herself laughing. Their conversation went from her church event, to the bible, Christian movies, sports, a godly relationship, and then the issue about her co-worker.

"There's this new lady in my store," she began. "She joined us about a month ago, but she's been upsetting me."

"Why? What happened?"

"Whenever I must talk to her, she says I'm rude, and even when I'm talking to some other people, she gets involved and still says I'm rude. I'm not a rude person; I'm a child of God. I'm very careful what I say and do. I'm polite and calm. I may be direct but not rude. As a matter of fact, I don't think anyone has ever accused me of being rude before, and it's making me feel upset."

"Did it happen again recently?"

"Yes, yesterday at work." She explained what happened.

"Really?"

"It has happened about six times in the one month she's been with us. And she looks at me with disdain. This is my second year in the store and I've never had any problem with any co-worker or customer. I'm a Nigerian graduate for crying out loud!"

"You have to tell her to stop it. Tell her you don't appreciate it but make sure you don't yell. Be calm but firm."

"I have done that, but she hasn't stopped." She explained. "I've even been praying about it and told my friends too because it's upsetting me."

"That's what satan wants to achieve – upset you. Don't give satan the pleasure."

"I know, and that's why I've been calm but I don't like what she's doing. The first time she said it, I thought it was both funny and embarrassing but now, it's obvious that she's trying to upset me. She's the rude one."

"Definitely. Well, I think you should just keep telling her to stop it. You will also need to be careful with her since you don't know what's on her mind ... and keep praying."

When the call ended and she checked the time on her phone, she saw that they had talked for about an hour and twenty minutes. She smiled. Talking to him was easy, and it made her happy.

A week after, she told him that the lady had quit the store.

CHAPTER 9

In the two months that followed, Eddie found that his thoughts strayed to Dami far too often, and he began to pray. *This lady is engaged! Why am I feeling the way I do about her? What's going on, Lord?*

He also discovered more things about her. Aside being a Christian who loved the Lord, a Nigerian graduate, and beautiful, she was a strong woman, hardworking, nice and caring. She also had zeal for the things of God and felt called to be in ministry, like him. All the qualities he was looking for in his woman.

Because he had said he wasn't looking for a relationship with her, and he knew she was in a relationship with Dapo, he had tried to keep his distance but couldn't.

Instead, he found himself looking for opportunities to see or phone her which was often. They met at the mall thrice, had dinner once in a restaurant, and he visited her at home twice. He noticed that she didn't wear much makeup anymore and he wondered if it had anything to do with him.

On the second Sunday of September, they went to the movies. There, in the lobby before they entered the theatre, he bought two bottles of soft drink for them, and a jumbo bag of popcorn for her.

"I don't really like popcorn." He told her.

He however ended up sharing it with her, dipping his hand in the bag as they watched the Christian movie.

Not that Dami minded sharing the popcorn with him. She liked it and liked how their hands touched as they reached for the popcorn. It made her head spin.

When he felt like holding her hands as they left the movies, he knew something was happening in his heart. He glanced at her. *Am I falling in love with her?*

Well, he would pray and try to get to know more about her. If God was involved, he would know soon enough.

****

Dami caught Eddie looking at her several times and realized she wasn't alone in the attraction she'd been feeling. She could tell that he liked her. She liked him too, but she had given her word to another man who didn't seem to appreciate her.

On the way home, she took a deep breath as she thought about the outing. She had never thought she would find herself in a situation like this. *Lord, have mercy*! I *will need to call Dapo and find out if we're still together or not. If we are, then we need to do something fast because we're drifting apart. As Stephanie had said, some things are wrong.*

The next day, she phoned him and asked, "Are we still together?"

"Of course."

"But I haven't been seeing you."

"I'm sorry but I've been busy." He said. "I had to travel to Ukraine at a time."

He promised to visit her at home on Thursday evening and when he came, she served him food and lemonade drink. She turned the TV on and sat across from him.

After some small talks, she decided to talk about her concerns, but he stopped her, giving her the I-don't-want-to-deal-with-this-right-now look.

"Dami, look, I'm here to spend some time with you. Let's not say things that would upset both of us or make me leave. Okay?" He stretched out his legs in front of him. "Let's just move forward."

"But how can we move forward if issues are not resolved," she said gently.

"They are not resolved because you refuse to let go!" He gave a slightly exasperated sigh.

"I refuse to let go because they have not been resolved." She pointed out, trying not to sound frustrated.

"Look, I'm not going to do this with you, alright?" He said, took the remote, and changed the channel. "If you have other things you'd want us to discuss, let me know."

She stared at him for some seconds, speechless. Then she took a deep breath and said, "Alright."

After that, they both tried to make conversations about other things and laugh but didn't quite succeed. They were like strangers. He eventually went home and left her feeling frustrated.

He phoned her the next day, but the call also left her feeling frustrated.

When in the days that followed, she found herself thinking more and more about Eddie, and comparing him with Dapo, she prayed more and wondered, *Should I end the relationship with Dapo*? As she continued in prayer, it became clear to her that a man who was not living right, and always giving excuses, could not be God's will for her.

She thought about Eddie. She liked him and liked the fact that he was a child of God. He had a good spirit and she felt very free with him, but she knew that the will of God was more important than her feelings. Even though she was happy with him, that did not mean he was God's will for her.

She knew however that if she was careful and listened to God, she would not make a mistake. *Who is Your will, Lord?*

****

The more time Eddie spent with Dami, the stronger his feelings for her grew, and the more he prayed. *I think I love her.*

He also searched his heart, to find answers to the many questions in his heart. *What do I love about her? How well do I know her? Does she have feelings for me? Do I stand a chance with her? Am I wasting my time or is God involved?*

He thought about the times they had spent together. They had enjoyed each other's company and he would have loved to say that she definitely had feelings for him but couldn't because she still had Dapo in her life.

He continued praying as he kept in touch with her and by the end of the second weekend in October, he was sure that he had found his bride. She was God's will for him, and he loved her. She had captured his heart. He wasn't going to rush into revealing his love for her though, as he wouldn't like another broken relationship. He would take his time to be sure of God's leading. She had not mentioned Dapo recently but that did not mean the relationship was over.

On the third Thursday of October, he phoned her to hear her voice and know how she was faring.

"Please let me call you back." She told him.

When she phoned back about fifteen minutes after, he asked, "Are you still at work?"

"No, I've just got home. I was trying to park my car when your call came in. How are you?"

"I'm doing well."

He told her about his day. Then he asked, "How was work today?"

"Actually, I didn't go to work today. I told you some time ago that I applied for a job in a company,"

"Yes, you did."

"I got a call yesterday to attend an interview today."

"What's the name of the company again?"

She told him the name. "I have a friend there. Please pray along with me."

He prayed immediately and promised to keep praying.

As they continued talking about the company, he searched for it on google. He exclaimed and said, "It's far."

"Yes, it is." She chuckled. "That's why I took the day off from work today."

"If you get employed, how will you get to work?"

"Well, I have a friend there, I will discuss with her. God will make a way. The pay is quite good. It will be worth it." She said and laughed.

On Sunday, he decided he would see her by Saturday to reveal his feelings for her. Dapo or no Dapo, he would have to let her know soon that he loved her, and trust God to work things out. He would not allow fear of rejection stop him. He began to plan what to say and how to say it.

On Tuesday, he received a message from her around noon.

Hi. I got the job.

He responded immediately.

Congrats. Will call you.

Thanks. OK. Still at work. I'll be home by 6pm.

Talk to you then.

He phoned her around seven in the evening and congratulated her again.

"I almost can't believe I got the job." She said, happy.

"That's the thing about Christians. We ask God to do something and when He does it, we're shocked." He stated.

They laughed.

"So, when are you supposed to resume?"

"I'm resuming in ten days' time, on the first of November."

"How do you intend to get to work? Drive down or ride the train or the like?"

"I've discussed with my friend, Ese. We'll rent a place together in that city."

What? She's moving away? "Rent a place?" He repeated, surprised.

"Yes."

He hid his disappointment and concern as he said, "Oh, okay."

"The next two weeks will be very busy for me." She stated.

"I can imagine. What kind of a place are you looking at?"

"Well, we're looking at a Townhouse with a basement. Favor's workplace is not far from the place and she wants to join us in the house."

"Wow! That's going to be a full house."

She laughed. "You can say that again."

"Victor is a real estate agent. Would you want me to tell him?" He wanted to know.

"Yes, please do."

"Okay, I'll tell him. He'll give you a call."

"Okay. Thanks." She said.

****

About an hour after, Dami's phone rang. She didn't recognize the number, but she answered it.

"Hi, Dami, this is Victor."

"Oh, hi!"

As they discussed, she found that he was very informative and attentive to details. She told him it was urgent, and he said he'd start working on it right away. He collected her e-mail address and at about midnight, he sent an e-mail to her, listing some Townhouses.

That's quite fast, she thought as she checked the e-mail. She sent a message to him on WhatsApp. *When can we see them*?

You can see them today if you want.

She forwarded the e-mail to Ese and Favor later in the day, and they agreed to meet on Thursday evening to inspect the houses. They met as planned and at the end of the inspection, they chose one and arranged for payment.

As she and Eddie were talking the next day, he asked her, "When do you want to move in so that Victor and I can come to assist you?"

"I'd greatly appreciate it. I'd like to move in on Sunday afternoon ... after church. I've told Stephanie and she's likely to come with Gabe."

"How much stuff do you have to move?"

"Not a whole lot." She said and laughed. "My brother said I can take my bed with me and the sofa set in the basement."

"Okay."

"Those are the heavy items, I think." She added.

"What about Favor and the other lady? When are they likely to move in?"

"Well, I'm not sure about them but I need to move in as soon as possible so I can be settled in before I resume work." She informed him.

She told him she'd need to buy some household items and groceries on Monday, and he volunteered to go with her.

After church service on Sunday afternoon, Eddie and Victor arrived at her brother's house with a rented truck. Stephanie and Gabe were also there, and soon, they had loaded the truck with her things, and were on the way to her new house. Her sister-in-law had put food in a food warmer, and they ate it when they finished unpacking.

Much later in the evening, she phoned her brother and his wife, and the four people who assisted her in moving, to appreciate them.

****

Eddie came to Dami's house the next day around noon and drove her to some stores to buy the items she needed. The weather was very cold, and they wore jackets. They returned to her house about four hours after. As they got down from his car, the door of the house next to hers opened and an African American woman emerged with a black dog on a leash. The dog started barking at them.

"Quiet!" The woman ordered the dog and without a protest, the dog stopped barking.

"That's a beautiful dog. Looks like a German Shepherd." Eddie said with a smile, looking at the dog.

"That's correct." The woman said proudly and smiled at them. "Do you have a dog?"

"No, I don't but I like dogs and know one or two things about them." Eddie said.

"I am Gabrielle. Are you the couple moving in here?"

He laughed and said, "No, no, she's the one." He pointed at Dami.

Dami smiled and said. "Hi, my name is Dami, and I'm your new neighbor."

"Oh great! I'm sure you will like this neighborhood. Where are you from?"

"I'm from Nigeria."

"Oh, Nigeria. Er ... the couple over there is from Nigeria." Gabrielle pointed at a building across. "Very nice people."

"That's good to know." Dami responded.

"Well, have a nice day."

"You do the same." Dami told her. "It's nice meeting you."

Eddie said goodbye to the woman, and she left with her dog.

As Eddie and Dami began to take the items inside the house, they talked.

"I didn't know you like dogs." She commented.

"I do. My family had one when we were in Nigeria."

When they were through, she took her phone and called a restaurant to order food for them.

"Good afternoon." The restaurant worker said. He mentioned the name of the restaurant and then asked, "How can I help you?"

"I'd like to make an order."

"Alright. For pick-up or delivery?"

"Delivery please."

"What would you like?"

She gave all the necessary details and about thirty minutes after, the food was delivered to her doorstep. She thanked the delivery man and paid him for the food, adding tip. The man left.

As Dami and Eddie ate, carrying a plate of food each, they enjoyed lively conversations and laughter. *Law and Order* was being shown on the TV that had just been connected to a cable in the morning.

He felt like telling her he loved her now but knew he shouldn't. He would have to be patient until the time was right. Now was not a good time, as she had a lot of things on her mind. Something as serious and life-changing as a declaration of love or a marriage proposal should be planned and discussed when there would be no distraction.

She needed to be emotionally present with him to process what he had to say.

He finished eating and left.

****

The week flew by for Dami as she unpacked her boxes and arranged her room and kitchen. On Thursday afternoon, her brother and his wife visited her and when they asked why they had not been seeing Dapo, she was forced to tell them that they were having some issues.

In the evening, she selected the outfit she would wear on her first day at the new job the next day. She put essentials in her black handbag, set her alarm, and by nine, she was in bed, ready to sleep.

She woke up at six-thirty in the morning, had breakfast quickly, and began to dress up. Soon, she left the house and arrived at the company about thirty minutes before nine when work was supposed to start. She exited her car, locked up, and approached the building.

Opening the front door, she stepped inside the tastefully furnished reception which had comfortable chairs and a center table that was piled with magazines. A lady took her to the office which she would share with three other people, and soon she was settled in behind her desk.

The day went well, and at five in the evening, she closed and headed home.

The next day, Saturday, Favor and Ese moved into the house with her.

The following week went by smoothly for her as she left the house in the morning at eight, resumed work at nine, and returned home around five-thirty in the evening.

CHAPTER 10

Dami and Eddie kept in touch on phone through calls and chats.

He wanted to know how she fared at work and she told him all about it. On the second Monday in November when she phoned him, he told her he would visit her on Saturday afternoon.

"I'll expect you." She said, happy. "Don't eat when you're coming. You'll eat here. I'll cook for you."

"Alright. I'll look forward to that."

On the day, he came carrying two bags of groceries, a bag of toilet paper, and a step-stool. The long sleeve beige sweater he wore on jeans had a mock neck and a short zip closure.

"These are for you and your friends." He told her.

"Aww, thank you." She said.

He put them down in a corner of the living room.

Favor was not at home, but Ese was in her room upstairs. She called her and introduced them.

"Meet Eddie. Eddie, this is Ese."

"Good to meet you." Eddie shook hands with Ese.

"And he brought these for us." She told Ese, pointing at the things on the floor.

"Wow! And a step-stool? Just what I needed." Ese said. She thanked him and returned upstairs.

Eddie and Dami sat down in the living room and after chatting for a moment, she invited him to the table to eat.

While they were eating, Ese returned to the living room, and sat down to sort out a box of documents.

They finished eating and joined Ese in the living room, talking, and laughing.

When he eventually left, Ese told Dami, "I think that guy loves you." She was stretched out on the sofa.

She laughed. "I think so."

"And I think you care for him too."

She didn't try to deny it but asked, "What do I do about Dapo?"

"You will need to make up your mind concerning him and what you want in life. If you've been praying as you said, you will know God's will soon." Ese assured her.

The following Friday, Eddie phoned her. "I'd like to see you this weekend if you're free."

"I'm free on Sunday. What's up?"

"I'd like us to discuss one or two things. I'll take you out for dinner."

"Dinner? You don't have to." She said. "Save your money -"

"I want us to."

"Okay."

In church on Sunday, Dami decided to ask Stephanie some questions about Eddie so she could know more about him, and Stephanie had only good things to say about him. She said he and Gabe had been friends for some time and Gabe trusted him.

Eddie arrived at about six in the evening. Favor was in the living room and she opened the door for him.

"Dami's ready. She will be down in a minute."

"Thank you." He said and sat down.

He had just started chatting with Favor when Dami came down.

His eyes scanned her from head to toe and he said, "You look great."

She laughed. "Thank you." It had taken her some time to decide what to wear. She eventually chose the light pink long gown and kept her jewelry simple.

She told him, "You look great too." He wore a black jacket over his shirt.

Favor was smiling.

She took her black jacket from the entryway coat closet and shoved her arms into the sleeves.

Shortly after, they left, and he drove to a seafood buffet restaurant. There, a waiter led them to a table, asked what they'd drink and provided it within minutes.

"Thanks." Dami told the waiter as she removed her jacket and set it aside.

Eddie blessed the drink and then he said, "I want us to talk first before we eat."

She looked at him.

With his heart pounding fiercely in his chest, he said, "There's something I'd like to say."

She sipped her drink without breaking the eye contact.

He took his phone, put it on silent, and set it aside. Taking a deep breath, he looked into her eyes and started, "Oluwadamimoola,"

Surprised to hear him call her full name, she laughed.

He smiled and went on. "It's a lovely name for a lovely lady."

Wondering where this was going, she smiled and gave him full attention.

"I'd like us to be more than friends ... I've fallen in love with you." There, he had said it. He felt relieved as his eyes searched hers.

"Oh, wow!"

"That's the truth. I love you ... very much." He said and took her hand. "I've been praying about you, about everything and I believe that you're the one for me."

She exclaimed again. Even though she suspected they were falling in love, yet she wasn't sure of what to say.

He went on. "You told me at a time that you were not looking for a relationship and I told you that I wasn't looking for one with you but that I was trusting God for one. I just wanted us to be friends."

She was still smiling, and he continued. "When I realized what was happening, I began to pray and ... I'm convinced that the Lord brought us together. You're the kind of woman I want; you're strong, simple, and sincere. You're also good and godly."

She opened her mouth to talk and then closed it back, still unsure of what to say.

"I'd like to be married to you, have children with you, and spend the rest of my life with you." He said, paused, and then asked, "Do you feel anything for me?" He silently prayed she would give the answer he wanted to hear.

She slowly nodded.

Halleluya! He waited for her to say more.

"Yes, I ... care for you a great deal. You've been a very good friend."

The way she said it made him think that a but was coming, and he wondered what that might be about. He braced himself as he waited to hear it. He would have to trust God to fulfil His promise to him.

"But ... I will need to pray and hear God concerning this ... concerning ... everything."

"That's okay. I just felt that you needed to know." He told her and released her hand.

She smiled again. "Thank you."

"Now that it's off my chest, can we go and get something to eat?"

They laughed.

He spoke again. "We can continue our conversation afterwards."

They stood and went to get food. When they returned, she prayed over the food and as they began to eat, they continued talking and laughing. He told her his plans and she asked him questions.

On the way to her house later, he turned on the radio and the car was filled with a Christmas song – Hark! The Herald Angels Sing.

"Wow, Christmas is almost here." She commented.

"Yes."

"I'll need to do my Christmas shopping soon."

"There's still time."

"I know, it's just that I don't like last minute shopping." She said, and added, "I love Christmas. It's my favorite time of the year."

At home, she told Ese and Favor about Eddie's confession.

"It's obvious that he loves you." They told her.

She also sent a message to Stephanie and Latrisha to inform them.

In her room, she phoned Eddie to know if he was back at home and he said yes. They ended up talking for about twenty-five minutes.

She got in bed and turned the light off. She lay in bed, silently thinking about the evening and Eddie. Knowing she would have to decide soon, she began to pray, *is he the one, Lord?*

In the morning, Eddie sent a message to her.

Good morning. Have a blessed day. Jesus loves you, and so do I.

She smiled and replied.

Thank you. Good morning and enjoy your day. We'll talk later.

At home in the evening, she called him to say hello.

"What are you doing?" She asked with a smile. Talking with him never failed to put a smile on her face.

"I'm on my way home from church."

After the pleasantries, he asked, "Have you started praying about us?"

She laughed and said yes.

He felt like asking about Dapo but told himself that he didn't have to. He didn't need to bother about that. They talked about God and themselves for about an hour.

When she was praying later and her mind went to Dapo, she wondered if she should contact him to end their relationship. This was the second time she would consider terminating their relationship, however, she counseled herself to wait and be sure of God's leading first.

To her surprise, Dapo contacted her on Thursday. She was at work, getting ready to leave for the day when his call came in.

Why is he calling me? She wondered, staring at the ringing handset. *Does he want to end our relationship?* She half hoped so, that way, she would not have to do it. She used to be afraid and worried whenever he threatened to leave her but not anymore. If he wanted to end it, now she was ready.

She ignored the call, not certain she wanted to do battle with him right now. It ended but her phone started ringing again almost immediately. Deciding to answer it, she told him she was at work and would call him later.

At home, she did.

"I went to the mall and was told you no longer work there. It was when I went to your brother's house that I was told you'd moved."

She was surprised. "You went to my brother's house? Did you want to see me?" She sat on the sofa and turned on the TV.

"Yes, I wanted to spring a surprise on you." He said. "How are you?"

"I'm fine." She answered dryly. "And you?"

"I'm doing well. I'd like to see you. Where do you live now?"

She mentioned the city.

"That's a little far. Why did you move?"

She told him she had a new job.

"You didn't tell me."

"You didn't ask me." She said, feeling upset again.

"Do you live alone or with a friend?"

"I'm sharing a Townhouse with two friends." *Why all these questions*?

"Oh, I see. Send the address to me. I'll come over. I need to see you. I've missed you."

What?! *Where's this coming from*?! She wondered. She had thought he wanted to end their relationship but here he was, saying he had missed her.

Unsure of how to respond, she said, "That's very interesting."

"Seriously. I'm coming to see you." He said and chuckled. "I'm sorry I haven't been around. Get ready to be taken out. Will tomorrow be fine?"

"I don't know. I'll have to check my schedule." She hedged.

"When should I call back to confirm?"

"I don't know. I'll let you know."

"Tonight? Tomorrow morning?" He wanted to know.

"Maybe tomorrow."

Her phone was beeping. It was Stephanie.

After the call, she returned Stephanie's call and said, "I was on the phone with Dapo."

"Dapo? Why?"

"I was surprised too when I received his call. He said he went to the mall and my brother's house to look for me."

"Why was he looking for you?"

"Well, according to him, he missed me and wanted to see me." Dami said.

"The guy is not serious."

Dami didn't sleep on time as she thought about Eddie, and then Dapo. *Why has he come back now? And what exactly did he want? Do I still love him? Do I want him?* She prayed to know what to do.

Just as she was getting to work the next day, she received a message from him. He wanted to know if he could come in the evening.

Well, he could come. She'd like to hear what he had to say. It might help her decide. Taking a deep breath, she sent a reply. *Yes.*

She received another message from him.

What's your address?

She sent it.

He sent another message. *I got it. What about dinner tonight?*

Did she tell him she was hungry? She thought, and rolled her eyes in her mind.

She replied. *No. I think you should come first. Let's talk.*

As she put her phone down, she didn't know what to hope for. Did she want him to say he'd realized his mistake, what a fool he'd been, and wanted her back or what? Could he have changed? If so, what should she do? And what about Eddie? *Lord, guide me!*

She screenshot her chats with Dapo and sent it to her friends on WhatsApp.

Latrisha responded. *People tend to realize what they've lost only after it's gone.*

Stephanie said, *Yeah, whatever,*
Favor responded. *It is well.*
Ese said, *I don't know about this.*

Dapo came at about seven-thirty in the evening, holding a small gift bag that contained a bottle of Dami's favorite perfume.

She thanked him and he sat down.

When she wanted to go to the kitchen to get him something to drink, he stopped her.

"Let me take you out, Dami."

She turned to face him. "We need to talk, Dapo."

"We can talk over dinner ... whatever you want us to discuss."

She shook her head. "I don't really want to go out. I'm not prepared to go out. Besides, I've had a very busy day."

"Three excuses at a go. Wow!" He said and laughed.

She didn't.

"Okay, I understand." He said. "We can go out some other time."

She went to the kitchen and soon returned with a tray that contained a can of soft drink, and a plate of two meat pies and two pieces of fried chicken. She set it down on the side table in front of him and sat across from him.

He stood and came to sit beside her. Taking her hand, he said, "I'm sorry."

She looked at him with a frown. "What exactly are you apologizing for?"

"Everything. I didn't give you enough attention for some time, and I'm sorry."

His words were confusing to her and she looked away from him.

He spoke again. "I also apologize about that other lady."

"You said you were only playing with her and that you didn't do anything wrong. Why are you now apologizing about it?" She wanted to know.

"Well, it upset you and upset our relationship. Let's try to fix things."

She remembered the past and how he had hurt her, and she felt the pain again. It still hurt.

As he talked, she didn't say much, checking her spirit to know what to do. He said things that should make her laugh, but she didn't, because she couldn't. She felt weighed down.

When he got up to leave at about ten, she thanked him again for the gift.

Later in bed, she prayed. Why did he come back? What about Eddie? *Holy Spirit, lead me and reveal the will of God to me.*

# CHAPTER 11

Eddie phoned Dami on Saturday morning and told her he would be coming later in the day.

"Okay." She was happy.

When he came, they began to talk, and then she said, "Dapo was here yesterday to see me."

He was surprised. "And what did he say?"

"Well, he said he missed me and apologized ... for everything. He wants us to continue."

"And what did you tell him?" He wanted to know.

"I didn't say much." She said truthfully.

He didn't ask further questions about Dapo so he would not appear to be putting pressure on her, but he knew he'd have to pray about this *threat*. God would have to help him.

When she woke up in the morning, she found a message from Eddie to wish her a happy new month.

She prayed and then responded to the message. Afterward, she got up to prepare for church, and soon, she and her friends left the house. After church, they went to some stores to shop for Christmas, and thereafter stopped at McDonald's to buy some things to eat.

Over the next three weeks, Dapo phoned Dami regularly, visited her, and took her to lunch. She was however careful around him, as the saying, "Once beaten, twice shy," kept coming to her mind.

She prayed about him, thought about all the parts of the relationship, and asked herself, what had changed? Had he changed? Could she trust him again?

The more she prayed, the more doubts she had about him, and she realized that she couldn't trust him again. Besides, she was not secure in the relationship, as she usually feared that he might drop her. No, she didn't want that kind of life. She wanted a man she would grow old with, and she didn't think she could have that with Dapo.

She also realized that she would miss Eddie if she let him go. She liked his looks, smile, and solid relationship with God. She also liked the way he freely talked about everything, and his tell-it-like-it-is way of talking. She loved him. The realization brought joy to her. She had to let him know and she phoned him immediately.

It was nine-thirty-five on Friday evening, two days after Christmas.

"Dami, hi."

Just hearing his voice filled her with joy. Yes, she'd made the right decision.

"Hi. What are you doing tomorrow? I'd like to see you." She told him.

"Okay. When and where?"

He came to her house at about one-thirty on Saturday afternoon and sat on the three-seater sofa.

She sat on a single sofa and said, "Thanks again for this." She pointed at the full-length portrait painting of her that was in a corner of the room. It was Eddie's Christmas gift to her while she gave him designer cologne by Giorgio Armani. "I love it."

"I'm glad you love it."

"Well, I've been praying about what you discussed with me." She began.

He saw that she was smiling and knew it couldn't be bad news.

She stood, came to sit beside him on the three-seater, and went on. "I've been searching my heart, checking my spirit ... and," she took his hand, "I want you in my life, Eddie. I love you." Her eyes were bright with love.

His expression changed to one of pure joy. *Thank You, Jesus*! He mouthed. Greatly relieved and happy, a big smile spread across his face.

"You're a wonderful man." She added.

He covered her hand with his second hand and asked, "What about Dapo?" He needed to know.

She shook her head. "I don't love him anymore. I don't trust him anymore."

"Have you told him?"

"No, I've just made the decision and wanted to tell you first. I will have to inform him. How do you think I should handle it?"

"Well, you can see him and tell him your decision ... that is if you think he'll be reasonable, and you'll be safe. But if you think he'll give you problems, then it's better you tell him on phone through a call or a message."

She smiled. "No, he's not violent ... or maybe I should say that I don't think he's the violent type. I'll see him and tell him."

"Alright but it has to be in a public place. Don't be completely alone with him." He advised.

"Okay."

He added, "I don't mind being there with you, in the background, in case you would need help."

"I'd want that, thank you." She said and then took her phone. "I'll call him now."

She tapped her phone and soon, she was talking with Dapo. "I'd like us to meet." She put the phone on speaker.

"Okay, I'll be there. I was just going to call you to say hi. Is everything okay?"

"Yes." She answered.

"What's this about?"

"It's just to talk."

"Okay, fine." He agreed easily.

"Can we do er ... Tuesday afternoon, around four?" She looked at Eddie for confirmation and he nodded.

"Tuesday? ... that's the last day of the year, right?"

"Yes." She said. Being the last day, she would not be working.

"Okay, it's fine." She heard Dapo say. "Am I coming to your house? Or better still, we can go to the restaurant we went the other day."

"No, no, no." She said immediately. "That won't be necessary. We can meet at er -" She looked at Eddie with raised eyebrows.

"The mall." He mouthed.

"At the mall." She finished.

They agreed to meet at the food court of the mall.

When Eddie left, Ese came to meet Dami in the living room and began to braid her hair. It wasn't finished that evening, and when they got home on Sunday afternoon after church service, they continued, and Ese eventually finished braiding Dami's hair around eight in the evening.

When Dami woke up on Tuesday morning, she decided to cook jollof rice and vegetable soup for Eddie and Victor, enough to last four days. By one in the afternoon, everything was ready and in food warmer to keep hot. She quickly had her bath and wore a top that had a Navy-blue design on a Navy-blue skirt that reached her knees. After packing her hair together at the back, she wore knee-high boots, took her jacket, and waited for Eddie.

He pulled up in front of her house at about two-thirty in the afternoon. She went outside to join him, carrying two food warmers.

He got down from the car and opened a back door for her. As she deposited the containers on the backseat, she told him that they were for him, and he could share them with Victor.

Surprised, he thanked her. He opened the front passenger door for her and waited to close it before going to the driver's side. On the way, they discussed the Watch-night service in their churches slated for later in the night.

They reached the mall a short while after, an hour before four when she was supposed to meet Dapo, and they walked around, enjoying one another's company.

They saw a shoe store and he led her inside, to the female section. They checked some shoes and she eventually told him, "The prices are a little on the high side."

"Okay but do you like any of them?"

"They're good but shoes are not my priority now."

"I'd like to buy one for you." He said.

She shook her head. "No, don't worry."

"I'd like to. You can consider it as my end-of-year gift to you."

"Wow! Thank you. Well, I think I'll want flat shoes. Most of my shoes have high heels."

They checked some shoes and eventually selected a black pair. She sat on the orange seat provided, to try them on.

"I'll help you." He bent down and assisted her to wear them.

"Thank you." She said, stood, and took some steps in the shoes. "They're okay."

She returned to the seat and sat down. He removed the shoes, put them in their box, and carried the box. They went to the payment register to pay.

They eventually went in the direction of the food court and as they approached it, she phoned Dapo to know where he was.

"There was a little traffic on the way but I'm almost there. I'm by the traffic light." He said.

"Okay. I'm there. I'll be expecting you."

She told Eddie. "He said he's almost here."

At the food court, they went to a restaurant and bought two cups of soft drink.

They carried their cups and as they walked away from the restaurant to the sitting area, she told him, "Thanks. We'll talk later."

****

"Let me hold this for you." Eddie took the plastic bag of shoes from Dami and she thanked him again.

He waited for her to choose a table, and after she had sat at one, he chose two tables away from her. He sat down, facing her, so that Dapo would back him. That way, he could be watching them without Dapo noticing him, and he would know if she would need his help.

As he looked at her, he smiled. *So, this is my future wife. I finally found her.* Who would have thought that they would get to this point on the day they met at Lakeworth Mall and sat beside each other at the movie?!

Soon, he saw a man approaching her table. *Is that him*?

When the man got close to her table, Dami looked up, saw him, and gave a little smile as she stood.

****

"Hi." Dami greeted Dapo.

"Hi." He responded and hugged her briefly.

"How are you?" He asked as he sat down, facing Dami, with his back to Eddie. "I'm sorry I kept you waiting. There was an accident involving two cars, and the police blocked the road."

"It's okay. No problem at all." She said.

He saw her cup of drink and said, "I need to get something to drink. I'm thirsty."

"That's okay."

"What will you want to eat?"

"No, I'm fine with this drink. Thank you." She said.

"Okay. Give me some minutes. I'll be back." He said, stood, and walked away.

She looked at Eddie and their eyes met. He raised his eyebrows questioningly.

She shook her head and smiled. Then her phone began to ring. It was Eddie.

"Is everything okay?" He asked in a soft voice.

She smiled, looking at him. "Yes." She said into the phone.

"Alright. Talk to you later."

"Thank you."

The call ended and she went on WhatsApp.

Soon, Dapo returned carrying a tray. It contained two disposable plates of Chinese food, and a cup of soft drink.

"This is for you." He gave her a plate of food.

"Oh, I told you I didn't want to eat."

"Are you fasting?"

"No, I just didn't want to."

"You can take it home if you want." He said.

"Okay, thank you."

He prayed over the food and drink briefly, and then sipped his drink. "You look good." He said.

"Thank you."

"How has your week been?" He took his fork.

"It's been good." She answered and decided she had to talk now before she'd chicken out. She wasn't here for pleasantries. "Er ... Dapo,"

He looked at her.

"I asked to meet with you." She began.

"Yes, you did."

"I've been praying about our relationship since all these days, and I prayed a lot more since about three weeks ago when you contacted me."

He listened.

She shook her head and stated, "I don't think we're meant for each other." There was no reason to beat about the bush.

He frowned.

"I asked to see you so I could tell you in person."

He put his fork down as his frown deepened. "Why? What happened?"

"As I said, I prayed."

"I love you, Dami,"

She shook her head. "I don't think so."

"Yes, I do."

"Dapo, you'll meet the right woman you love soon, whom you will be committed to."

"If it's because of the other issue, I've said I'm sorry." He said.

"I've forgiven you but that's just one of the issues. I thought about everything."

"Let's give this a chance, Dami."

She shook her head again. "It won't work."

"It will. We can make it work."

"We could make it work if we were meant to be together, but I don't think so."

Then he asked, "Is there another man in the picture?"

She could have easily denied it and said no, but being a Christian, she hated lying and she would not do it now just to please him. She wanted to say, *yes, there he is behind you*, but she knew she shouldn't involve Eddie in this matter.

She told him, "There was no other man all along but when these issues came up, I met another man who loves and appreciates me."

"So, there's another man,"

"Now, yes." She confirmed.

"Who is he?"

"You don't know him."

"What's his name?" He pressed on.

"That's not necessary because what we're discussing is not about him."

"It's about him."

"It's not and you know it." She said firmly.

"Is there anything I can do to make you change your mind?"

She shook her head. "No, you don't need to do anything."

"So, that's it?"

"Yes, it is." She carried her handbag.

"Wait, Dami, let's talk."

"I need to leave now."

"What about your food?"

"I can take it with me unless you'd like to have it back." She said.

"No."

"Then I'll have it." She carried the food and her cup of drink. "I wish you all the best, Dapo."

She stood and as she left the table, she looked in the direction of Eddie and their eyes met. Knowing that Dapo might still be looking at her, she didn't talk to Eddie but walked toward the hallway. She was sure that Eddie would follow her.

He did.

At the hallway, she looked back and saw Eddie behind her. She glanced behind him, and when she didn't see Dapo in sight, she stopped and waited for Eddie. He reached her and they continued walking, toward a door that led to the parking lot.

"How did it go?"

"Well, I've told him. It was obvious he wasn't expecting the news." She said.

"Did he try to persuade you to stay?"

"Of course, like every normal man would do. He apologized for the chats and said he loved me, but I made him know that it's over. Then he asked if there's another man in my life."

He smiled. "What did you say?"

"I said yes."

His smile broadened.

"But I didn't say more than that. What should I do with the food he bought for me?" She laughed.

"You can eat it." He said. "After all, you didn't ask for it. Also, he bought it right there at the food court, so it's safe to eat. Bless it and eat it."

They reached his car and entered. As he pulled away from the spot, he said, "I've told my parents about you. I'd like us to get married in the new year, around July. I want us to start our life together as soon as possible. What do you say?"

"Yes." She was happy. "I want that too."

"Oh, and, let me wish you a happy New Year in advance." He took her hand and gave it a gentle squeeze.

"Same to you." She responded with a smile, feeling a big relief in her heart. A new and better chapter had opened in her life.

Eddie took a CD which was a collection of Christmas hymns, inserted it in the car's CD player, and turned it up just loud enough.

She rested her head against the back of her seat and sang along.

O tidings of comfort and joy,
Comfort and joy,
O tidings of comfort and joy.

****

Eight months after, on the last Saturday of August, Eddie and Dami got married at *Loving God Pentecostal Assembly.*

Note from the author

I brought up the issue of infidelity in *Life Goes On*, and this book, *When A Man Loves A Woman*, to encourage you, dear reader, to be faithful to God and your relationship or marriage.

God has not changed His mind about infidelity; it is still a sin. He has not changed His plans for His people; they are good plans, '...to give them the expected end.'

I hope this book will challenge you to do what is right, and when heaven or the society asks, "Who is on the Lord's side?", you will stand and say, "I am on the Lord's side; I stand for Jesus!"

It's All About You, Jesus!

ABOUT THE AUTHOR

Taiwo Iredele Odubiyi is a Pastor and the Executive President of TenderHearts Family Support Initiative, a Non-Governmental Organization. She has a deep and strong passion for relationships and expresses this in ministries - nationally and internationally to children, teenagers, singles, women and couples. She reaches out to these groups through counseling, seminars and programs such as Teenslink, Singleslink, Coupleslink, and Woman to Woman.

Married and blessed with children, she is the regular host of the TV and Radio program - It's all about you!, and Tenderheartslink on YouTube.

This is the twenty second of her soul-lifting and life-changing novels.

I love hearing from the readers of my books. If this book has blessed you, send your comments to:

WhatsApp: USA: +1 443 694 6228
Website: www.pastortaiwoodubiyi.org
Facebook: Pastor Mrs. Taiwo Odubiyi
Twitter: @pastortaiwoodub
Instagram: @pastortaiwoiredeleodubiyi

If you have friends and loved ones, then you have people you should bless with copies of these very interesting and life-changing novels and books.